W9-CBH-709

THE RAGING CURRENT!

The white-canvased wagon swayed in the middle of the Pecos River, tossed about by the churning waters. Cole arrived at the bank, lashing the reins on the palomino's flanks to have it charge into the river. Jane saw Major Perry pulling the harness of the front horses, his own mount barely able to keep its head above water. The boat-shaped wagon floated but appeared about to tip any instant.

"Turn 'em upstream," Cole yelled at Jeffers. He then waved at Perry to guide the horses into the current, just as a ship would steer into the wind. The major, with only a hold on one of the horses, couldn't alter the course. Lapping waves, splashing in the faces of man and animal, added to the confusion.

With the water at her knees, Jane stopped upon realizing she too could be swept away. Then she saw Cole, submerged to the waist, screaming and whistling, left hand full with the palomino's mane, forcing the horse past the wagon on the downstream side, whipping the team one by one with just the reins of his own mount. When he reached the front horses, he too grabbed their harness. With him at one side and Perry at the other, the two riders led the team closer to the far bank.

Within just yards of land, rider and horse slowly emerged from the river, followed by each pair of the team. The right wheels erupted through the surface. A scream within the wagon focused Jane's attention on Adela, who was thrown to the side and crashed into the inner wall. A black bundle flew over the side. An instant later, Adela's violent cries confirmed Jane's fear. It was the baby, Joaquin.

Other *Leisure* books by Tim McGuire:
NOBILITY
DANGER RIDGE

GOLD
OF
CORTES

TIM McGUIRE

LEISURE BOOKS NEW YORK CITY

*To all my teachers, both formal and casual, who instilled in
me an appreciation of the past.*
I was listening.

A LEISURE BOOK®

June 2000

Published by

Dorchester Publishing Co., Inc.
276 Fifth Avenue
New York, NY 10001

If you purchased this book without a cover you should be aware that
this book is stolen property. It was reported as "unsold and
destroyed" to the publisher and neither the author nor the publisher
has received any payment for this "stripped book."

Copyright © 2000 by Tim McGuire

All rights reserved. No part of this book may be reproduced or
transmitted in any form or by any electronic or mechanical means,
including photocopying, recording or by any information storage
and retrieval system, without the written permission of the
Publisher, except where permitted by law.

ISBN 0-8439-4729-2

The name "Leisure Books" and the stylized "L" with design are
trademarks of Dorchester Publishing Co., Inc.

Printed in the United States of America.

Acknowledgments

To the staff at the Grand Prairie Public Library for their help in the research. *Muchos Gracias*, to Edgar Carranca, Max Reyes, and Ernie Perez with the Spanish dialogue. A hug to Jenny Jones, my biggest fan and promoter, and thank you to the many people I have met and have taken the time to convey their kind words toward my stories; you keep me going. And, as always, a special recognition to the members of *DFW Writer's Workshop*, who must bare the brunt of the blame for my success.

GOLD
OF
CORTES

Prologue

He came from out of the sun.

Adela shielded Joaquin from the rider's view with the shawl. She held her son close to her bosom so the infant would feed and not cry.

A black hat shaded the rider's eyes, but his face was unfriendly. Dust covered his shirt, which the sunlight showed to be green. His pants were the same color as the parched sand, but dark leather wrapped both legs from the knees to the boots. A pistol was tucked in a holster strapped on his right hip and a knife was sheathed on his left.

He turned to her cart and the fallen right wheel pinned under it. She had no tools to repair it, nor the ability. She risked asking for his help. *"Usted puede ayudar?"*

He shook his head, put his hand to his

mouth and spoke the language of this land, which she never learned. He swung his right leg over the blond horse's head and slid off the black saddle. Both boots landed at the same time, making a loud thud and a spray of dust. He took a lariat from the saddle and started for the cart, but first he spoke again and pointed at the cart, then at her.

She feared she knew what it meant. His price for the work was her. She had known men like this, but had never given herself. The water in the last jug was very low. If she didn't get out of the desert, her son would die from the heat and she of thirst. He was too big to fight. Fate had made her choice and she meekly nodded.

In little time he had tied the rope to the cart and his horse, which together with her tiny burro pulled it upright. He put the wheel on. A shaved piece of the cart wood was hammered in place as a new pin. Her journey could resume.

He came to stand in front of her. She laid Joaquin on the cart and stretched the shawl over the child's head. Adela unfastened the final three buttons of her blouse and opened it to show him her milk-swollen breasts, then bowed her head to let him do his will. The sun stung her uncovered chest, but she knew it would be the least pain she would endure.

She quivered when he reached for her. He gripped the blouse. She waited for it to be ripped from her shoulders. Instead, he pulled it back over her and shook his head. Her heart pounded harder when he stepped toward

Joaquin. He took the shawl from over the baby. She would take his knife to kill him if he reached for her child.

The stranger lifted the shawl and pointed to its sewn emblem: a knight in armor.

Chapter One

"When God thought up Hell, he had Texas in mind." Clay Cole viewed the plain while recalling John Holliday's words, which never told more truth. Wilted brush strewn about waves of sand stretched to the horizon. Even the prickly pears yellowed from the sun's daily barrage. Orphaned twigs from passing tumbleweeds crackled under the palomino's hooves. Winter likely had been a brief relief, but it had left no signs of rain, and spring only meant the worst of summer was on the way. Not even clouds could stand to stay here long.

Although appearing more a girl, the light-skinned woman rumbled over the terrain, patient with her burro's meager steps. Cole followed her lead to the south and tried to remain hopeful she understood what he wanted.

He didn't often trouble himself with people's reasoning, but her traveling alone through the heart of western Texas seemed a foolish act. Bringing a suckling child along made the mistake worse. The purpose eluded him. Pondering it kept him from noticing the vast empty land ahead.

Without a quick answer, he soon was reminded that he himself was only a few feet behind her. He snickered upon recalling another favorite notion: fools like company. A glance at an old yucca made him wonder when last he'd seen a cholla. A wandering path had taken a good piece of his time, most of his money but not all of his memories.

Although at one time the tall cactus had surrounded them, they became a rare sight as this journey continued, just as the buffalo had during the last ten years. The beasts' numbers lightened not from nature but from the greed of Easterners moving west. A greed he shared during the journey from anxious youth to veteran soldier.

Months before, as he had closed in on the border, his desire to escape an unfair reputation had faded. He did not know the local lingo, and Mexico was full of outlaws with deserved reputations. A stronger desire to one day clear his name had turned him from south to east.

Two winters went by before he crossed the Rio Grande into El Paso. The town had changed since he first saw it. Not long after it had become part of the Texas frontier, card cheats and cattle rustlers began seeking out the border haven. Now it seemed the law had taken root; a Texas Ranger had turned marshal, and iron rails would soon bring further settlement.

Train tracks brought to mind the place where he thought he would settle. That memory now jabbed his gut like a sharp knife. Once, when he'd nearly been part of a family, unwanted fame as a gunhand had cost him the chance of being the head of a household in Nobility. He knew from the start the delight of living with Ann, Evie and Noah Hayes would never have lasted long. To let them live in peace, the Rainmaker left New Mexico at the same time the railroad swept across the territory.

He touched the red bandanna which was knotted around his neck. He had not looked back in more than a year.

"*Mira,*" the woman said while pointing to what appeared to be a roof on the horizon.

Cole spurred the palomino, careful not to get too far ahead of the woman or make himself a target for a shooter nervous at the approach of strangers. The structure had been white but was now stained with grime, making it look gray. Once he saw it billow with the arid breeze, it was clear it was a tent the size a full-grown man could walk in and out of. He'd seen this first in the States War when he was a boy and later when he was a trooper. A tent this big was normally meant for a commander.

He rested his right palm on the holster of his Colt .45. A slow amble brought him within sight of two other tents of similar size. A long table with chairs sat outside the first tent. Four horses nibbled on the sparse grass and weeds while reined to a line. An old prairie schooner sat near by. Its arched bows had no cloth cover. But what concerned him most was the absence of whoever owned this camp.

A glance behind showed the woman still driving her burro without a hint of worry. As he turned back around, a buzz passed his ear followed by a loud cry.

"Fore!"

Cole drew the Colt and pointed it in the direction of the cry. A pop in the dust to his left had him cock the hammer and fire, splintering small bits of wood and cloth into the air. The crack of the shot echoed three times through the plain.

"I say, are you injured?" came a voice from his right. Cole quickly re-aimed the pistol at a man emerging from behind a small dune. The stranger climbed over the dune with the help of a peculiar-looking cane. The end was wrapped in leather and the handle was of forged metal. "I say again, are you injured?"

Cole shook his head.

"How fortunate. I feared the worst when I saw you in my line. Terribly sorry." The bearded man came closer; that he was grinning while a pistol was pointed at him seemed just as peculiar as the cane. "I'm afraid you have no need for that, sir." He opened his light-brown waistcoat. "I'm unarmed." He came to the side of the palomino and offered his hand.

Cole eased the hammer in place and holstered the Colt, bewildered by this man's actions.

"Nigel Apperson is my name. Fifth Earl of Westchester, member of Parliament and loyal servant to Her Majesty."

Cole didn't understand what was meant but habit had him take the man's hand. "Clay." He hesitated, remembering a name that helped him hide in New Mexico. "Hayes. Clay Hayes."

"A honor, sir." Apperson said and took a step back. "I don't suppose you've seen my ball, have you?"

Cole slowly peered at the hole in the sand on his left. He faced Apperson, who looked at the same hole then smiled at Cole.

"Oh, dear. Well, I suppose that's all for today." He turned around toward the tents. "May I offer you something to drink?" He took off his checkered cap, revealing gray hair, and fanned his face. "This heat is most unbearable. Please, join me."

With an aching thirst and without any cause to worry in sight, Cole dismounted and followed behind Apperson, leading the palomino.

"Beautiful steed, if I may say. I admire your taste, Mr. Hayes."

The remark made Cole remember that he'd exchanged the horse for a man's life. At the time it seemed a fair trade, and he never was comfortable with being thought a horse thief. Besides, it would never take the place of a favored Appaloosa he had to lay down in New Mexico. This one didn't seem like a man's mount, and the Mexican black saddle and bit were too fancy, but they came with the horse.

The Mexican mother had stopped the burro and was soon greeted by a red-haired woman emerging from the first tent. The two hugged like long lost sisters. It appeared the gamble of following her had paid off.

"You know her?" asked Cole.

"Oh, my yes. Adela had been traveling with us."

Both men came to where the women still stood jabbering.

"Dr. Jane Reeves from Boston, may I present Mr. Clay Hayes," Apperson said and he then embraced Adela and looked fondly upon her child. The red-haired woman in a long heavy skirt and white blouse offered her hand, which Cole gently took.

"Mr. Hayes, it's so nice to meet you." Her words didn't have the same cut as Apperson's, but she did have the same manners and her tone reminded him of another Eastern woman.

"You talk Mex?" asked Cole.

She nodded. "A little. Does that surprise you?"

He cocked his head. "Up until a year ago it would have. But now, I guess I got no call to be."

"Adela tells me you rescued her from the desert."

"A hero?" Apperson said with surprise. "How magnificent. What an even greater stroke of fortune for us that you happened by."

"Well, I saw she was in need of help. And when I saw the patch she was wearing, I figured I'd make her a deal."

They all appeared confused, so Cole pointed to the shawl's emblem.

"Oh," Apperson said. "The coat of arms. Of course."

"But, if I may ask," the woman said, "why would that interest you?"

"That's kind of a long story. But, the short of it is, I met a man named John Holliday in Nobility. He said you was looking for those who could handle guns to lead you into Texas."

"Mr. Holliday. You don't say." Apperson seemed pleased at the mention. "Charming fellow. I'd wished I had longer to spend with him, but I met him on the day of our departure from Denver."

"He gave me this." Cole pulled from his pocket a small card that had the same design as the emblem and handed it to Apperson.

"Yes, indeed. I gave it to him then. Pity he couldn't join us himself." He gave the card back to Cole. "However, perhaps it was your good fortune to come along," he said with a smile.

At a shuffle of footsteps Cole slid his hand to the butt of the Colt. A balding man of similar age and dress to Apperson came from the corner of the tent. Apperson held out his palm.

"No need for alarm, Mr. Hayes. This is my man, Jeffers."

The balding man nodded. "Terribly sorry to have startled you, sir."

Cole thought for moment. "He's your what?"

"A gentleman's gentleman."

Cole felt his jaw slip open.

"Jeffers is my employee. He looks after us

here, sees to the meals, cleans the clothes, that sort of thing."

Cole pushed his hat back and shook his head.

"He's Lord Apperson's butler, Mr. Hayes. Is that troubling to you?" said the red-haired woman.

"This all seems a mite strange."

"How so?"

Cole huffed out a deep breath. "I come across this Mexican woman who's wearing this that's belonging to you. She leads me back to here where no white man should be. She don't talk English good, but you talk to her in Mex." He looked at Apperson. "You nearly cut me off my horse using that cane. Both of you act like you should be back East. You got a man that does all your cooking and cleaning, and pardon me for saying, ma'am, but you're a doctor and woman to boot."

All of them chuckled at him.

"Well, I assure you, I'm able to handle both duties with little trouble, Mr. Hayes. But you may be confused by my title. I'm not a medical doctor. I'm an archeologist."

Cole repeated the unfamiliar word to himself. "If you don't treat people, what do you treat?"

"Well, it's a bit complicated."

"Yes," Apperson interrupted. "I can see Mr. Hayes's point. This all must appear odd to someone of his ilk. However, just as he said, it's a long story. I suggest we all rest the subject for conversation while we dine. Jeffers has prepared a meal of local fowl. Shall we?"

Cole glanced at the setting sun, still not knowing what he had let himself into. But the smell of meat drifted by him, and his empty stomach drew his attention to his first cooked meal in six days. Listening to what they had to say seemed another fair trade.

Chapter Two

Jeffers set the last plate of roasted quail in front of Cole. Everyone kept their hands in their lap, while the manservant went back into the main tent. It took a glimpse at the first star of the clear night to remind Cole his hat wasn't needed. He removed it and dropped it to the side. Jeffers returned with a dark bottle and placed it in front of his boss.

Apperson poured a small amount of red liquor for himself and the two women. "Do you care for any wine, Mr. Hayes? It's French. I've been saving it for just such an occasion."

Cole noticed the women waiting for him to decide. He thought it polite to join them since the liquor didn't appear the same color as corn whiskey. He nodded and Apperson poured him the same amount.

"Well, then. Let us toast a successful expedition." Apperson and Dr. Reeves raised their glasses. Adela did the same upon seeing her friends' actions. Cole picked up his glass, which signaled the other three to take a sip. He followed their lead, and cringed at the tartness of the wine. He smacked his lips. "It tastes like squeeze."

Apperson chuckled. "Yes, it takes some acquiring." Once the glasses were set down, everyone but Jeffers began their dinner. Apperson was the first to finish his mouthful. "So, Mr. Hayes. You said you were from New Mexico. Do you have family there?"

Although the question punched his gut, Cole took no offense and shook his head.

"I see. Then, how did you know Mr. Holliday? I gave him that card in July of 1879, almost two years ago. I've returned to England since then," he paused. "To gather investors."

"Him and me were in the same saloon at the same time."

"Ah, a saloon. I've missed the conversations in the taverns at home. You'll forgive me, Jane, but there are certain places where women should never tread."

"Oh, there were women in this one," said Cole. His eyes darted to Dr. Reeves, catching the glow of the distant fire silhouetting her face. "But not like the present company."

She smiled as she took another sip from her glass.

"And that's where he gave you my card?"

Cole nodded with his mouth full. Before he

swallowed, the baby's cry prompted Adela to jabber Mex at the doctor and made Apperson stand. She left the table and Apperson took his seat.

"What she doing out here? She don't look old enough to be up this late, much less out on her own."

"Adela, unfortunately," said the woman, "is estranged from her family. She told me her father banned her from his house after she married a man of whom he didn't approve. An even worse tragedy is that her husband, the child's father, was killed by bandits. We met her in San Antonio and she traveled with us until she said she couldn't go further west. I believe she said she has an uncle near San Angelo."

Cole took another bite when Apperson spoke. "Yes, well, you were talking about Mr. Holliday, Mr. Hayes."

With his throat clear, Cole continued. "He said something about you being an English fellow and that you were traveling through Texas needing men with guns. It brings up a matter I think I should make plain right now. I don't run folks off their land or rob no banks."

Apperson grinned. "Neither do I. No, Mr. Hayes, my reasons for needing men familiar with firearms and this land are completely legal."

"Well, then if I'm to think about hiring on with you, what is it you're after way out here?"

Apperson first looked to Dr. Reeves then back at Cole. "I suppose you've a right to know. Don't you agree, Jane?"

She paused before answering. "Certainly. We couldn't expect anyone to consider it without knowing all the facts."

"Very well, then, I'll tell you. However, to understand the scope of the matter, I'd like to ask you a few questions. Are you a student of history?"

Cole thought for a moment. "I ain't had much book learning, if that's what you're meaning."

"In that case, perhaps I should start with a brief lesson so as to explain the magnitude of our objective."

Figuring he was in for a story, Cole put down his knife and fork.

"Oh, please, go on with your dinner. Would you like more wine?"

Cole shook his head.

"Well, then I'll begin with the reason for our conquest, as it were," Apperson said, glancing at the doctor. "Long ago, some three hundred and fifty years, a man came to this side of the world in search of riches. He was a Spaniard. His name was Hernán Cortés. A bit of a rogue as a youth, Cortés left from home in Spain and arrived on an island that is Cuba today. There, he grew restless and bargained his way to the head of an expedition to the mainland from a friend of his, a chap named Velázquez, who was the viceroy of the New World on behalf of the king of Spain."

The aroma of the bird convinced Cole he could take another bite before it became cold and listen at the same time.

"Once his ships came upon the mainland shore, Cortés, who was still a young man, felt it important to earn the confidence of the men who had joined him, mostly investors. And he had his own ambitions to one day rule the region, thus he sent off one ship of small treasures back to the king to seek the title of viceroy of New Spain. Some of the men protested, swearing a loyalty to Velázquez. And so, to convince them to press on," Apperson said as he cut another slice of meat and plunged his fork into it, "he unloaded the ships and sunk them in the harbor."

Eyes now wide, Cole replied, "Seems like a damn fool thing to do."

"Brutally." Apperson chuckled with delight.

"That's exactly what his men thought at the time," Dr. Reeves said. "But that way they had no choice but to follow him."

She folded her hands together onto the table just like a teacher at a school desk. Cole never looked forward to lectures, but he never had a teacher with such smooth skin. Her blue eyes were equally distracting, so he looked at his plate and took his last bite to get his mind straight on what she said.

"Cortés was a man of considerable guile."

"Of what?"

"Guile. An ability to act in one's interest without revealing the purpose."

"Like a cardplayer?"

"Exactly," she said, pointing her finger at Cole and smiling. "Just like a cardplayer. And it served him well as he marched deeper into the jungles of Mexico."

Cole shook his head. "There ain't no jungles in Mexico."

"In this area maybe not, but further south, it is a mountainous terrain full of wild plants and animals, and also wild people at that time."

Cole looked at Apperson in bewilderment. "I'll have a mite more wine now." The Englishman graciously poured a small amount into Cole's glass as she continued.

"The natives were quite glad to see these foreign men and sought the Spaniards' help in fighting the Aztec empire, which dominated the area. Despite some resistance as he went from tribe to tribe, Cortés was able to march to the largest city he had ever seen. The Aztec capital, Tenochtitlan."

"Where?" Cole asked and slurped the wine.

"Mexico City, today."

Cole shook his head once more and held his glass out for more wine. Apperson filled it to the brim. "I heard of that place. My pa said he fought there in the war with Mexico. What's this got to do with me?"

"I was coming to that," Dr. Reeves said. "The Aztec leader was named Montezuma. At first, he had tried to buy off Cortés with small gifts of beads. But, when he and Cortés met, he began treating all of the Spaniards with great regard, adhering to long superstition that a bearded god with light skin would return from the east. And since some of the men were on horseback, a sight the natives had never seen, they thought these invaders to be gods. Cortes took full advantage of this and began tearing down all symbols of Aztec religion, replacing them with crosses and images of the Madonna. When the people revolted, Cortés put their ruler in chains."

"Yes, but there is the matter of Velázquez," Apperson added. "You see, he didn't entirely trust his young friend Cortés and so sent another expedition shortly after with orders to find Cortés and arrest him. Narveaz, a rival conquistador, was sent. Upon hearing the news of more ships coming from the east, Cortés is believed to have hid his personal bounty, which he claimed."

Unsure if the wine had clouded his memory, Cole put down the glass. "What was it that he claimed?"

Apperson leaned back in the chair and removed two cigars from his vest pocket. Sliding one smoke under his nose, he broadly smiled as he offered the other to Cole. "Fabulous treasure. Brilliant masterpieces of bejeweled gold. Some handed down from Montezuma's own family and dating back to the Mayan culture, possibly over a thousand years old."

Cole bit off the end of the cigar and spat it to the side. Both men lit their smokes with the table candle.

"Do you see now our interest, Mr. Hayes?"

Cole nodded but was still confused. "You haven't said why you're here. With all this treasure you're talking about, how come you ain't in Mexico City where you say it is?"

"The very point why we are here, my good

fellow. The Aztecs had long plundered their neighbors and feared the same fate. Being the marvelous people they were, they knew the logic of hiding their wealth away from possible seizure. Rumors of hidden treasure have long been dismissed, since none was ever found or its loss accounted for. I've even heard of lost gold in the mountains of Arizona." Apperson chuckled. "More wine?"

Cole raised his open palm and shook his head. "I'm having enough trouble understanding what you're saying. This fellow Cortés sure seems to talk these people out of their money easy."

"Well," Dr. Reeves smiled, "he did it with the help of a woman."

Leaning closer, Cole raised his eyebrow as the woman doctor went on.

"She was given the Christian name of Marina. She was a gift from her adopted father, one of the native chiefs, and although she was bestowed to one of the other Spaniards, Cortés quickly claimed her for his own. While learning his language in short time, she also bore him a son."

After cocking his head to the side, Cole asked, "She talked them out of the money?"

"Hardly," Apperson answered. "She wasn't well thought of by the Aztecs."

"Yes, that's true," Dr. Reeves said. "She spoke a language mostly used by the neighboring tribes, ancient Mayan, known as Nahuatl. She convinced those tribes to join Cortés and his men to overthrow the Aztecs. History has marked her with another name for her actions. *Malinche*. It means 'traitor.' "

The word threw Cole back in his chair. "Traitor?"

"Yes, does that shock you?"

It had been a short time since he had heard the word that had followed him around like a hovering buzzard. Visions of the Little Big Horn, Custer and charging Lakota warriors flashed in his mind, but he shook them away with an answer. "I know what it's like to be accused of something that ain't right."

A momentary quiet held the table until Apperson continued. "History often isn't right, Mr. Hayes. It is widely believed that the treasure that Cortés had smuggled out of the capital was put upon a ship, perhaps one of those of Narveaz, whose men Cortés had also convinced to join his forces. However, the bounty never made it back to Spain and is presumed to be at the bottom of the sea due to a storm and beyond the reach of human hands forever. But I differ with that account."

"And that's why you're here?"

Apperson nodded. "Precisely. Cortés had developed a fond relationship with Montezuma, quite unbelievably, indeed. He was told by Montezuma of a secret place where treasures were stored in case of attack. In the panic of the threat of arrest, Cortés had his hoard taken to the cache. But none of the Spanish knew exactly where that was. It remained a secret. Until now."

Cole took a slow drag from his cigar, as did Apperson.

"I am a collector, Mr. Hayes. While in London I came upon a document worth collecting only for its historical value. It is a letter from Hernán Cortés, then summoned to Spain, to his illegitimate son, Martin, who was still in Mexico. The text is a jumble of languages, I assume for secrecy, describing a sanctum three hundred leagues to the north." He smiled at Dr. Reeves. "No one knew at the time exactly what it said. I sought out the advice of experts, which brought me to Jane, here."

"I read the letter," she said. "It tells of a great deposit of antiquities hidden away. The letter describes an area of great desolation where a chamber is located, guarded by the spirit of the Aztec god Tonatiuh, the god of the sun and warriors. It is said that this spirit can make the air burn like brittle wood if the treasure is disturbed. But there are many such stories."

"Quite right," Apperson blurted. "So many, in fact, another seeker of fortune, named Francisco Coronado, came upon legends of a great city made of gold, which lie to the north. He never found any gold, only the adobe huts of primitive Indians. But his travels expanded the empire of New Spain, later, of course, to be known as New Mexico." He refilled his wine glass. "Cortés himself searched for the treasure, finding only the western coast of northern Mexico and the Pacific Ocean. Rumors of harbored riches abounded during his tenure as governor, and his activities were closely watched. When

Coronado was given the right to pursue the lost cities of gold, Cortés sailed to Spain to complain to the royal court. He never returned to Mexico. That's why we are here."

"How's that?" Cole asked.

"I'm not anxious to attract attention to our expedition, thus the need for men as yourself who don't need attention brought to you. I am willing to pay five hundred dollars for your services, Mr. Hayes, in addition to a five percent share of the value of our findings to lead our party and insure our safety."

Cole looked at both of them, still unsure of what was being asked of him. "Where we going?"

Apperson swirled the wine in his glass and looked first to the woman doctor, then back at Cole. A smirk wrinkled his face.

"We are off to the hunt, Mr. Hayes. For the fortune of a lost civilization. You see, I don't believe Coronado was so naive to search for mythical cities of gold. It is my belief that he was looking for the gold of Cortés."

Chapter Three

Dawn peeked above the eastern horizon. Cole enjoyed the cool air against his bare chest, knowing its gentle brush would soon be gone, but the throb from the red liquor hours before would likely stay with him most of the morning. It wasn't the only thing troubling his head.

Of what he remembered was said, it seemed all a blur of lectures and foolhardy talk of looking for something that nobody was sure where it was. However strange, it wasn't the first time he heard it. Many a man had lost everything digging for ore in some far-off place, sure of finding his fortune. Some, if not most, also lost their lives. Gold fever had never settled into his blood. Now wasn't the time to be chasing after that which wasn't firmly in sight.

He thumbnailed a match to set fire to the gathered wood and dry scrub in the firepit. Flame quickly licked the brush aglow and warmed away the chill from his fingers.

Another prospect bothered him. The future. It too was a blur of what to do next and what not. Had he continued on into Mexico as intended there was no guarantee of any peace much less any prosperity. The army wouldn't follow him over the border, but that would leave him in a land without knowledge of the lingo among those who didn't take to outsiders.

And once there, how long would he stay? Being thought an enemy of his own country would keep him out of it for the rest of his life, unless he faced the charges he knew had already been decided. A life on the run had cost him any peace he thought to gain by avoiding jail. Perhaps it was time to stop running and drop the heavy weight carried for the last five years.

If Mexico was at the bottom of America, at the top was Canada. When he was a trooper, he rode near its border, trying to keep the Lakota from escaping. All he knew about the place was that it was full of Indians and miners. But he heard English was spoken in some parts. It may make for a new home, but it would take much of a year and saddlebags of money to make the trip.

He glanced at his saddle. He was offered 500 dollars for a simple job. Scouting for a cattle drive had paid him thirty dollars a month for an entire summer ten years earlier. Besides the considerable bounty, this time he wouldn't have to smell those miserable animals or listen to them bawl while he tried to get shut-eye. The only risk remained in collecting what was promised. It wouldn't be the first time he had to draw his pay directly from a boss's pocket, mostly with the help of a pistol. And he'd not think twice about doing it again.

He snickered as it occurred to him that if he really meant to talk himself out of hiring on with these folks, he wouldn't be staring at that saddle, due to it being strapped to his horse heading south or north. He often decided what to do by not making decisions he didn't want to make.

"Good morning, Mr. Hayes."

Cole faced around to Dr. Reeves. Her skirt hung beneath the shawl wrapped around her shoulders. "Morning, ma'am." The cool breeze along with her stare turned his bare skin cold. He scrambled to pull on his shirt.

"It's beautiful," she said, peering at the sunrise.

"It is this time of day. About the only time it doesn't pain you to look at it. I was going to set the coffee to boil."

"I'm sure Jeffers will see to that."

"No need to bother him. No point to wake him for me."

She smiled and approached him. "You certainly are an early bird."

"An old habit." He piled more wood on the fire. "When you was raised on a farm, you get used to starting the day before the sun does. Came in handy when I was in the army."

She came closer to the fire and held her palms open. "Have you thought about our offer?"

"I was just pondering that," he said, looking into her eyes. "How likely are you thinking it is we'll find this Cortés's gold?"

Her eyebrows raised as if surprised by the question. "That's very hard to put into words. It's reasonable to presume we may not find it. The letter is very old—a treasure in itself—but who knows if what is said in it is true or if it will lead us to the find."

"Do you have this letter? I'd like to see it."

"Oh, my, no. It's much too fragile an item to be here."

"Then, if you don't mind me asking, why are you out here?"

She looked to the dirt but quickly raised her head, blinking her blue eyes and pointing her finger before she spoke. "Imagine something of yours that you might think to be of little value. What would it mean to someone to discover it three hundred years from now? It isn't just the valuables, such as the gold and jewels, it's all the remnants of a people who lived before your parents and grandparents were ever born that hold the true value."

He stepped to the table and lifted the cloth cover to find the shiny metal coffeepot. All the while he listened to her.

"It's quite an enormous endeavor, really. Should we locate it, I'm unsure what we will find, but I know I will feel like I've touched another world."

"How you mean?" he asked, lifting the pot's lid. The interior sparkled as clearly as the outside. "Damn," he muttered.

"What I mean is," she said as she looked to the dirt, "discovering artifacts from another time, another civilization is significant alone for me. It's all I hope to gain from all of this. It would be like traveling through time itself."

He banged the lid on the pot.

Her head jerked up. "Is something wrong?"

"Ah, no. I just was looking for some coffee before I head out, but it looks like that man, Jeffers you call him, cleaned the pot."

"Yes. Well?" she asked with a puzzled expression.

"Ain't one thing you never clean, and that's a coffeepot. It gives the coffee the taste of saddle soap and it takes near a month to get back what was cleaned out of it." He walked over to a large wooden barrel and opened the lid. He took a ladle and dipped himself a drink, then closed the lid. "You said that just touching this gold is enough to for you. I'd bet Apperson has a different look at it."

"Of course." Her quick answer carried not only conviction but also a dab of scorn. "He's a man who admires the potential value in objects as well as their beauty. He's a businessman. This expedition has considerable expenses, and he is entitled to profit from his investment."

"Yeah, well, I've known men who loved smelling money, but none quite the same as he does it."

"Yes," she answered with a giggle. "He is a bit eccentric."

"Loco is more like it."

She looked away for an instant, then shook her head at him. "You said something about leaving?"

"Yeah," he said slurping from the ladle. "You got less than a full barrel of water. We can't start after nothing until we know where there's more." He tipped the ladle over his mouth and emptied it. "I figure it'll take me maybe two days at the most. There's a few small water holes west of here, or there was once. It's been some years since I seen them last."

She smiled slowly. "You said 'we.'"

He nodded. "That I did. I can't say this is what I thought I'd be asked to do. The idea is plumb foolishness. But I got nowhere to go. And whatever place I end up going to will cost a patch of money. So I figured I'd hire on." He walked to his saddle and picked it up. He led the palomino near the fire, glancing at her occasionally while throwing the blanket and saddle atop the mount. "I was hoping to tell Apperson, but I need to get a better start on the day. I guess I can leave that to you."

"I'll be sure to do that."

With the cinch tight, he climbed into the saddle. "I should be back by tomorrow nightfall. Tell everyone to sit tight till I get back."

"We'll be waiting," she said with a smile. He returned it and tipped his hat as he spurred the horse.

* * *

Heat distorted the air rising off the sand. Even shadows wavered directly under that which made them. Cole raked his sleeve across his brow, but sweat soon returned to dangle and drop to sting his eyes.

He stopped the palomino's lope, pulled off his hat to release what felt like steam off his scalp, wiping the sweat once more. Another swig from the canteen left him with little more than half and after he was through dribbling handfuls to the horse, the time had come for him to find another source before day's end or turn back to Apperson's camp under the cool of night.

Arid air was difficult to breathe. A dust devil stir would be a welcome relief, even if just to change the constant bleary sight of mound after mound of scrub and sand. The bleak surroundings rekindled thoughts of heading south, but he had told the woman he would be joining up with them and he wouldn't mind seeing her face again upon his return.

A twist about in all directions produced the same view, until a wisp of white smoke drifted above a small rise to the northwest. He was sure the vision was no mirage, for it didn't waver and it hung much too low to be the lone cloud of the sky. He remounted and turned the palomino for the rise. Once at its crest, a small shack roof with a stovepipe protruding through was within a mile.

Nearing the shack, he could see it was a dugout with a roof leaned into a rocky mesa no higher than the mound. He slowed his approach upon sighting four lathered horses reined to the brush next to the dugout. His right hand slid to his holster, as he knew men with tired mounts usually were running from something.

He didn't recognize any brands or saddles that would concern him, and his thirst pushed him off the palomino to rein it into the brush and take a cautious walk down the steps and into the dugout.

The door creaked as he entered. All eyes came his way with the sunlight beaming into the small earthen cantina. He closed the door and soon felt the cool difference of the shade. A moment was needed to adjust to the meager light of six candles suspended above the room's center by a wooden support. One step put him at the end of the bar. The portly barkeep seemed to be Mexican, but the man spoke Texas English with no accent. "What'll you have?"

Liquor had never squelched a scorched thirst. "Water will do for now." Random chuckles ebbed through the room.

"No rivers run in here. Whiskey or tequila?"

"In that case, I'll take in the shade."

"Mister, I don't run no parlor. If you want to stay, you buy a drink." He put one hand below the bar top. "If you don't, you leave."

Cole slowly turned to see three men at the nearest table interested in his decision. Any rest would come at a price. Dispensing silver rather than lead seemed the proper manner. "A cup of tequila," he said, facing the barkeep. A dented tin was pulled from the shelves behind the bar and the portly man filled it from a keg slid into the dirt wall.

"Two dollars."

"Proud of it, are you?" Cole said, drawing a pair of coins from his pocket to the bar.

"Yup. It was stilled two weeks to the day."

After an initial thought of cleaning his pistol with the clear liquid, Cole reluctantly sipped the liquor, which burned a trail down his throat. "It tastes fresh," he coughed.

The barkeep's grin lacked three top teeth.

"Since I'm a customer now, I was looking for any information about water holes and the like within a ride west of here."

A shaken head was the reply. "I'm not a mapmaker."

"Me neither," gritted Cole, leaning closer to the bar. "But I have been known to be grateful for politeness in the past."

The portly man bobbed his head with new respect. "I don't know all the spots around here. But take a seat and I'll ask."

A single empty table sat near the outer wall. Cole ducked under the low beams and took one of the chairs. The barkeep went from table to table like a butterfly to spring blooms. Another sip of the tequila produced the previous result. It needed to be his last if he was to keep his senses. Cole attempted to rub the lacquered taste from his tongue onto his sleeve when a boy not more than twenty gleefully pulled up a chair.

"How do?" the freckled youth said. His dark hair was long and curled in waves, and it jutted out from a short brimmed hat. He spoke just as cows chewed with the lower jaw not meeting the upper. "I heard you're wanting to know what's the west of here," he said, extending his hand. "My name is Billy."

Hesitant before accepting the young man's hand, Cole thought again about his own name. "Call me Clay."

"Hey, I heard of you," Billy said loud enough to fill the room. Cole's heartbeat quickened and he pulled his hand away to palm his holster once again. Aware of interested ears, Billy leaned closer to whisper, "You're from New Mexico. I'm from New Mexico myself. Lincoln County to be exact. Nice to meet you, Mr. Allison."

"I ain't him," growled Cole.

"I understand," Billy said with a wink.

"I don't think you do. That ain't me."

Billy's grin showed he didn't believe him. "Then what name do you go by?"

"I'll answer to Clay. That's all that need be just to get some friendly information."

"Okay, Clay," the kid said with seriousness. "And since we're now friends, I'm going to tell you what you want. Providing you can do me a little favor."

"We ain't friends."

"Why? I like you."

"I don't like you. Tell me what you got to tell me or leave me be."

Billy slumped back in his chair. "Why, here I was going to tell you where there was water."

"And where might that be?"

"No more than five miles from here. A hole cut into the rocks was filled up by a storm about ten days ago. Should still be some fresh water in it. But . . ."

"But what?"

"But you better be careful, 'cause I also saw some unshod tracks in the sand when I came through there."

Cole paused in thought. "Apache ponies?"

"Could be. None were present when I came through. But you know water holes. Everybody needs use of them."

"In what direction?"

"Now, see," Billy said shaking his finger at Cole, "that's where that favor comes in. Really, I'd still be doing you a good turn, because I'd be willing to lead you to where it was. It's hard for a fellow to remember everything without seeing it again."

There normally was one reason men offered to be a guide. "How much?"

"Oh, I wouldn't be asking for money," Billy said, glancing at the table where the other three customers sat. "At least, I wouldn't be asking now."

The dim light showed all the men covered with dust. The nearest was the biggest, with a sombrero, bushy beard and a single bandolier looped across his paunch. Across the table sat a man whose whiskers and gut weren't as thick. A dark hat with white oval studs showed he wasn't one used to long days in the desert. The last of the trio seemed the youngest and the most nervous, with frequent glances at Cole. The hogleg strapped to his hip appeared too heavy a weight for such a slim frame.

Cole looked to the sheepishly grinning Billy. "Ain't my feud."

"I'm not looking to fight. Just for a friend to walk out of here with."

"Are you wanted?"

"Well," Billy said with a slight laugh, "you could say that. I had me a little trouble in Lincoln County. But it weren't my fault. Everybody there has me in a bad mind. I ain't the man they say I am. They keep picking on me. Do you know what it's like to have folks say things about you that aren't true?"

The question took a spot in Cole's head. "If you're a robber or murderer, I don't care to have you with me,"

"I'm none of those. Look at me. Would you think me a killer?"

"What piece do they have in you?"

Billy shrugged then giggled and shook his head.

After a deep breath, Cole looked at the three men then at Billy. "I need you to show me this water hole before much more light passes. There are some people sorely needing it and I got to get them to it."

"I'd be glad to ride along. Where are they headed?"

"That ain't your concern. I just need a guide to the water."

Billy nodded. "Let's ride." He and Cole rose from their chairs, triggering the other three to rise also.

"Where are you going with him, mister?" asked the big man.

"Why does that concern you?" replied Cole.

"Your friend there is Billy the Kid, wanted in Lincoln County, New Mexico. Shot a lawman and escaped from jail not more than two weeks ago. There's a thousand dollar bounty on him, and we mean to take him back for it."

Billy showed a blank stare as if surprised by the notion.

"How do I know you telling the truth?" Cole asked.

The big man gripped his holstered sidearm. "You don't need to know. We've been tracking him for six days and the bounty is ours. That and this I'm holding is all the proof you need."

"I ain't looking for trouble. You tell me where there's ample water around here, and I'll let you have him."

"We don't have to tell you nothing, mister," said the youngest one. All but his gunhand and hogleg was obscured from Cole by the center pole. "We'll just take him." He drew his gun.

Billy grabbed a liquor bottle, smashed it against the table and thrust the jagged edge into the young man's throat. A gurgled scream filled the cantina.

The big man twitched for his pistol. Cole lifted his knee and drove his boot heel below his attacker's paunch, sending the big man backwards to collapse a table.

44

The one with the studded hat shoved a knife at Cole's belly. Catching the man's hand with the steel point inches from his gut, Cole forced the blade into the wooden post, then grabbed the thin bearded man's nape and rammed his nose into the pole. Cole then reared his heel against the man's boot, felling him like a tree to the dirt floor.

The big man scrambled forward, throwing chairs from his way. Cole twisted about to swing his leg level with the sombrero's brim, jabbing a spur into the big man's neck. Anguished cries splattered with the blood as the sombrero flew off. The bandoliered paunch crushed a chair into the ground.

A hooting laugh brought Cole's attention to the smiling Billy. "I do like you," he told Cole.

Billy's smile instantly shrank with Cole's grasp of his collar and the immediate point of the Colt's barrel.

"I said I don't like you. I want none of your troubles." Cole's voice quivered. "Tell me now where the water is or your head comes off."

"Five miles," stammered Billy. "You see some rocks to the west. Head for them and follow the runs lined in the sand. You'll find it."

"I don't know who you are," said Cole shaking his head. He clubbed the Colt into Billy's scalp and Billy slumped to the floor. "And I don't want to." As he turned for the door the barkeep quickly raised his empty hands. Without further threat, Cole took his anger out on the door and stepped into the sunlight.

45

Chapter Four

Once the roan strode atop the rise in the sand, a lean-to shack cradled by a small escarpment became visible. Upon a slow approach, activity became more evident. A Mexican of stocky build dragged bodies out of the door. When the roan came to stand yards from the shack, the Mexican, unperturbed by the advance of a stranger, gave only a glance then continued with his work.

"Good afternoon."

The Mexican looked up again. "It wasn't for these folks. Are you here for him too?" His English was clear as he pointed at a young man who squirmed on the ground while rubbing the back of his head.

"I'm afraid not. Who might that be?"

The stocky man shrugged. "I don't know and

don't care. These other three were here for him, and for trying, one got killed and the other two don't look to live long." He looked around and took a longer stare. "If you're not here for them, then what is it you're after? Don't see many army fellows out here."

"I'm Major Perry with the Seventh Cavalry," said the officer as he dismounted. "Right now, all I'm looking for is some water."

"You got any money?"

Perry shook his head.

The Mexican's eyes darted to the Schofield-model Colt revolver tucked in the major's belt. Then he bent and searched the pockets of one of the men on the ground, a burly man with blood staining his neck and the side of a bushy beard. The major scratched his own of similar ragged length, remembering the time when his pride in an officer's appearance was one of his priorities. He brushed some of the dust from his soiled sleeve.

The Mexican drew two coins and stood. "I'm too tired to argue. He won't miss them. There's a water barrel under the bar inside."

"I'm grateful for the hospitality," Perry said as he started for the shack. He stopped at the feet of the squirming young man. "I would have judged this fight to have a different outcome. You say he did this to the three of them?"

With a quick shake of the head, the Mexican responded, brushing his hands. "Nope. I didn't say that. Another fellow did this."

Four men lay on the sand, all with open

wounds and only one showing a sign of life. It was a sight which brought memories, and a guess as to who could have conquered such odds. "Do you know who he was?"

"This one here," the Mexican said, again pointing at the one squirming. "He called the man Clay."

A chill shot through the major, as he staggered closer to the Mexican. "Clay Cole?"

The question brought another shrug. "I don't know. All he said was Clay."

Perry bent over the young man on the ground. He gripped the kid's collar, trying to penetrate the oblivious daze. "You there, listen to me. What was the man's name who did this?"

The reply came with groans and squinted eyes. "What? Who are you?"

"Just tell me! What was the man's name who did this to you?"

"It was Clay. Clay . . . Allison. I think it was him."

"Allison? Are you sure? Not Cole? Who's Allison?"

"Clay Allison, a mankiller. I think it was him. He wouldn't say his name, but I'm pert sure it was him. Who are you?"

Perry released the collar with a shove. "That doesn't concern you. What did this man Allison look like?"

"Well . . ." The kid paused to rub his head. "He was a big fellow, tall, big shoulders, a scar running down his face, dressed in green and wore a big black hat."

"That's him," Perry nodded. "Which way did he go?"

"I don't know and don't care," said the Mexican. "After he done in them two, he didn't look like he wanted anyone to follow him and I didn't want to get my head blown off looking."

"Water," the kid muttered.

"You'll get water when I get my answer." Perry remarked.

"No. Water. That's where he's heading. He said he was leading some folks, and he needed to know where there was water."

Perry knelt beside him. "What did you tell him?" When the answer wasn't immediate, Perry grasped the collar again and shook the kid. "Where, damn you? Where did you tell him to go?"

The kid's eyes bulged and his voice came as stammered huffs. "Five . . . miles, West. I . . . told him . . . about a hole . . . in the rocks."

With the information he needed, Perry rose and marched to the roan. As he mounted, he swung the horse to the west and spurred to a gallop.

The Mexican's final words faded into the drifting dust. "Don't you want the drink?"

Dark streaks in the solid rock widened with each step of the palomino. Moisture made the small chips glisten like sparks as he passed. A last step to the top of the hill revealed a pool no bigger than a width of a house, but the bottom couldn't be seen. Cole reined the horse into the water. Once at the center, the surface lapped at the animal's girth. It proved an ample supply to steer the party toward. After better than an hour's ride, it appeared the kid who called himself Billy had told the truth.

Cole unfastened his gunbelt and hooked it around the saddlehorn. As his horse drank, he slid into the cool grip of the pool. The chill brought a quick shiver, but soon the soothing relief had him sink to the shoulders. He dipped his hat into it then tipped a deluge onto his sweltered scalp. While he lay back to allow his sore neck some comfort, the glare off the water seeped under his closed eyelids. There wasn't much day left.

He trudged ashore, allowing the horse to soak its legs a little longer. The mild breeze on wet clothes provided further reprieve from the afternoon's heat. He wiped the hair from his face and tucked it under the hat. While doing so, the white of a feather tucked in a crack of the rocks caught his eye.

When he pulled it out, he noticed it was a tail feather. White shaded with brown and gray. Gauging by the length, it seemed to come from a hawk or perhaps an eagle. Although possible, those with this coloring and size weren't often found in this region. The idea that the bird it had belonged to wasn't the one that left it reminded him what Billy had said about unshod ponies.

A clack on the rock spun him around to find a figure knelt behind cover aiming a pistol at him. He slapped his side for his own, but there was no feel of iron or leather. A glance to the palomino showed his Colt revolver snugged in the holster around the saddlehorn.

"Put your hands high where I can see them."

Cole's eyes and ears told him at once who was holding a gun on him. He complied with the order. It wouldn't be made again by the man who had made it a personal duty to bring him back before a court-martial. "Is that you, Miles?"

"You keep your hands there. I won't be fooled by your tricks anymore," Perry said as he rose and approached.

"How's that shoulder? I could've put that slug in your heart had I wanted to."

"Perhaps you should have. It would have saved both us years of grief."

"Well," Cole remarked with a snicker, "if it's what you want, I can still oblige you."

"Quiet. Where is your sidearm?"

Cole reluctantly pointed to the palomino.

A smile grew on the major's face. "That's not like you, Cole. A man can get killed with such carelessness."

"It must have been the heat. Did you steal that Schofield? That ain't no army issue. Last I left you, you didn't have a gun. Did that Mac-Gregor fellow loan it to you in New Mexico?"

"Not your concern at the moment, I wouldn't think. All that matters is that I have it now," Perry answered while keeping the gun barrel at his side steadily pointed at Cole. "I've spent a long time thinking of this moment, with you as my prisoner. All those days following your trail, realizing what this day would mean."

"And what's that?"

"Redemption!" Perry took a deep breath and his eyes appeared to glisten. "Nearly two years, that's what it has meant. Two years since I sacrificed my career to pursue you in the name of justice."

"I've been telling you all along that I didn't do what's claimed against me."

"That's not for you to decide. The army will decide your guilt for your part at the Little Big Horn."

Cole shook his head, memories again swirling in his mind. Soldiers' painful screams, arrows and bullets ripping into their bodies. "There ain't nothing I forgot."

"I'll bet not. I would think you would remember the deaths of over three hundred men you were responsible for."

"It ain't the truth. I told you that before."

"Quiet!" Perry ordered pointing the pistol at arm's length. "I'll not trade words with you anymore. That time will come. All I need decide now is your return to Fort Lincoln."

For Cole, there was another decision to be made. "What if I ain't going?"

Perry shook his head. "The way I see it, you don't have a choice."

"I got a choice," said Cole, staring at the gun.

Still silence gradually gave way to the muffled pounding of horses hooves. Cole looked in their direction. Four horsemen emerged through the wavering heat. He squinted hard to focus on the lead rider. As they closed in, a glint off the chest meant the reflection of metal, which indicated who they were.

"Rangers," muttered Cole.

He glanced to Perry, who seemed unsure what to do next. Then a small grin grew on the major's face.

The riders slowed their horses just in front of the rocks. The leader wore a brown coat and hat, white shirt covered by a striped vest that matched his pants, the legs of which were tucked into tan boots. Black hair sprinkled with gray brushed over his ears. His mouth was partly hidden by a long thick mustache. He pulled his pistol and aimed it at Perry. "Drop the weapon."

The major's grin turned to confusion. "You don't understand. I'm Major Miles Perry of the United States Army. This man is my prisoner."

"No," the ranger said while cocking his pistol. His three companions drew their iron and did the same. "It's you that don't understand. I'm Captain Chet Burroughs of the Texas Rangers, and I told you to drop your weapon."

After a moment, Perry tossed the revolver to the ground.

"You're both under arrest."

"What for?" both Perry and Cole asked.

"For busting up a cantina, killing three men and beating up another," Burroughs said and stared at Cole from head to toe. "And any other crimes the both of you may have committed in the past." He pointed the pistol at Cole. "What's your name?

Perry answered, "His name is Clay—"

"I didn't ask you," Burroughs chided, silencing the major.

The name he'd given to Apperson seemed the best to Cole, but Perry knew otherwise. Lying might spark further trouble. "The name's Cole. Clay Cole."

"Cole?" Burroughs asked. "I heard it was different."

"Then you heard wrong. That's my name."

"I can attest to it," Perry added. "He's a traitor to the army, and I'm here to take him back for court-martial. His name is Clay Cole. But you may be referring to another name he's better known by." With all the rangers listening intently, Perry faced Cole. "He's the Rainmaker."

The party of rangers all looked among themselves in bewilderment. "Is that true? Are you really him?" Burroughs asked.

A deep breath allowed Cole a moment to ponder his answer. The name given him by a Pawnee squaw upon his birth had become a brand for trouble that had chased him from New Mexico and kept him outrunning a reputation for most of the last five years. No matter the trouble it was about to cause, he nodded to the ranger in memory of his mother, who bragged about the name with great pride.

Burroughs dismounted and slowly walked to him with gun still drawn. Once the barrel was at Cole's belly, Burroughs holstered the pistol and offered his hand. "It's a honor to meet you."

Startled by the friendly action, Cole took the man's hand.

"Do you know who he is, Captain?" Perry asked with scorn.

"Yessir, I do." Burroughs faced the major. "I know the name of the Rainmaker is known all around these parts as the only one who stood up to the Corbin gang when they were rustling cattle down over the border."

"That was a while back," Cole said with a smile.

"People here still remember you. Ever since you chased the Hensley brothers out of the county. Never seen them since."

The mention of the outlaw pair brought the recent memory of the trouble the brothers had brought Cole in Colorado, and how he had left them there with a bullet apiece between the eyes. "They won't be back."

Perry threw his hat to the ground. "This is an outrage! As an officer of the United States Army, I demand you arrest this man and place him in my custody."

"Reconstruction is over, or haven't you heard? We don't take orders from Yankee blue bellies anymore," said the ranger captain, shaking his head. He turned back to Cole. "I was fixin' to arrest you on account I was told you might be Clay Allison by the boy back at that cantina. I don't have call to, but I figured he was up to no good. But, seeing it's you, I guess I'll have to let you go."

"I'm beholden to you for that," Cole replied with a grin.

"What about the men he killed at that cantina?" Perry yelled.

"Thems are bounty hunters," said Burroughs walking back to his horse as Cole waded into the pond after his. "I got no stomach for their kind. The proprietor said they drew first and they got what was coming to them. A hazard of their business."

"They were after the kid that told you I was Allison," Cole said, leading the palomino from the pool. He strapped his gunbelt on. "They said his name was Billy and he was wanted back in New Mexico."

"Well," Burroughs said, mounting his horse, "this is Texas. As long as he don't cause any further trouble here, I haven't the time to chase him back there. I got to get back to leading these young fellas after a band of Comanches that have been raiding cattle and burning houses."

Cole froze. "Comanches?"

"Yup. They staked out a territory west of here, but they stay on the run so often, I can't seem to catch up with them."

"I got a party of city folk looking to head west," Cole muttered.

"You better turn them back. This bunch is mean. Cut open a farmer and his wife just enough to take a day to have them bleed to death. We found them after they been out in the dust for a week. Poor souls. That's a message that they'll do the same to anyone that comes their way."

Cole took a deep breath, understanding the warning all too well. A distraught Major Perry caught his eye, then Cole faced the ranger captain. "What about him?"

"I got no reason to keep him and don't want him even if I did." He chuckled. "Ain't legal to shoot Yankees no more. He's your trouble now, friend."

Cole walked to Burroughs's horse and offered his hand. "I thank you again for what you did. I'll tell the folks I'm with they need to turn back."

"A pleasure, Mr. Cole," Burroughs replied with a wink. "I just wished I could do more for you. You tell them folks they need to leave them Comanches to us. As spread out as they've been raiding, I can't say I'll be able to offer you help should they give you trouble."

"Understood." Cole nodded. Burroughs turned his horse away from the rocks and led the other rangers away at a gallop.

Cole looked again at his old foe. Perry appeared ready to scream in frustration, his eyes darting to the grounded Schofield then back at Cole, who drew his Colt and shook his head. Although the thought of leaving the major without a gun or horse came to mind, another one crept into Cole's head. Comanches were the worst Indians alive. And he had been accused of letting Indians slaughter soldiers. A lie that would be more believable if he left Perry as an easy prey. He picked up the Schofield while keeping the Colt pointed at the major.

"Get on your horse."

Chapter Five

Although cloudy night skies made the trail back to Apperson's camp hard to follow, keeping sight on Perry riding a few feet ahead was more of a challenge to Cole. Even with pistol drawn, a wary eye had to be maintained. An ambush from a hidden weapon could appear at any time. The truth be told, Cole wouldn't have minded or attempted a shot should the major gallop off into the dark.

The act would be Perry's will and would clear Cole's conscience if in two days time the uniformed body was found plugged with bullets or arrows. At least it would shed Cole's mind of one concern. However, the major had kept his horse in line with the Colt's muzzle since nightfall and stayed the same course now with the first signs of daybreak. There was no need to worry.

He was guiding the man who had hunted him along his own planned escape. The simple answer would be to end the officer's pursuit with a slug in the back of the head. But it would be a guilty man's answer. The increasing light brought the question to an easier conclusion. Although at gunpoint he could set Perry off on a safe route toward the nearest town, the better idea was an old one, to keep an enemy in plain sight.

A campfire shone like a beacon against the dim dawn horizon. As they rode closer, Cole took a deep breath in anticipation of the reaction to his guest's arrival and announcement.

"Hello in the camp," he called. The woman doctor and the manservant both came from their tents. He waited until she waved them in, despite Cole's knowledge that they had no reasonable defense to repel invaders.

Her welcoming smile was first to catch his attention. "I didn't expect you until later today. I see you've brought a friend." Both Cole and Perry glanced at each other. The smile shrank when her eyes dipped to the drawn revolver when Cole dismounted.

"I wouldn't say I'm a friend, madam," Perry said, tipping his hat. "I'd say I'm a captive."

She looked to Cole with bewilderment, then back at Perry. "But you're with the army, aren't you? I don't understand." Before Cole could answer, a bellowing voice came from behind.

"What have we here," said Apperson as he approached from his tent, wearing a robe, trousers, riding boots and a purple scarf tied in a fluff around his neck. "Oh, good morning, Hayes. Good to see you again."

"Hayes?" Perry said loudly, staring at Cole. "Are you still using that name?"

All eyes fixed on Cole as he grunted his throat clear. "There's a story that goes along with that."

"Please tell us. I know I for one would like to hear an explanation," Dr. Reeves said with a distrustful stare.

Cole looked to her and glimpsed the same expression on the Englishman. "Well, you see . . . um," he began. "All right. I'll just say it. He's right. My name ain't Hayes."

"Well, just what is it, then?"

"His name is Cole," Perry tersely announced. "Clay Cole. He's a traitor to the United States, for which I've been tracking him down since I learned of his whereabouts almost two years ago."

"And you are, sir?" Apperson asked.

"Forgive me," the officer said while tipping his hat once more. "I'm Major Miles Perry, Seventh Cavalry, Army of the United States."

Dr. Reeves kept staring at Cole as if in shock over Perry's charge.

"So, Major Perry," Apperson said while taking a silver cup from the matching tray carried by Jeffers, "what was the treasonous act this man committed?"

"He gave information to the Sioux Nation

that led to the slaughter of over three hundred troopers led by Colonel George Armstrong Custer."

The expression of sadness and horror on the woman's face took away some of Cole's breath. He wanted to explain, to say anything, but all the words came at once into his head and jammed in his mouth only to come out as mumbled gibberish.

"I see," Apperson said, breaking the momentary silence. "Mr. Cole, or Hayes, whatever you consider yourself, is this matter going to prove an impediment to perform your duty?"

The question seemed just as much gibberish as what was in Cole's head. "Huh? How you mean?"

"Are you going to honor your commitment to the expedition, man?"

"Well, I need to talk to you all about that."

"Just yes or no, we've not the whole day to discuss this."

Out of a habit of charging ahead once he was backed into a corner, Cole blurted his answer. "Yeah, I'm going to come, but I got to tell you something."

"Good. Jolly good. Well, since we've got that sorted out, I'm in the mood for breakfast. Would anyone join me?" Apperson turned for the main tent, but Perry's shout stopped him.

"I don't believe what I've just heard. I told you this man is wanted by the United States Army as a traitor, and you're asking him to breakfast?"

"That's precisely what I'm asking him to do,

Major. When I first spoke to this man one of the conditions of his service was whatever his past, it was not a concern of mine, as long as he would faithfully abide by his duty as a guide to my party. His role in your accusation isn't a matter for my judgement. Now, if you'll excuse me, I detest cold eggs."

The fire in Apperson's words lit up Perry's face. He dismounted and marched in front of the Englishman. "Sir, as a gentleman, you must observe the laws of this country."

"Major, as a gentleman, you must observe my right as a guest in this country not to dabble in matters beyond my control. By what I can see," he leaned to peer at the Colt in Cole's hand and the absence of one in the soldier's, "you're in no position to arrest him, am I correct?" Perry's frustrated sneer at the truth served as his answer. "And I'm sure there is a point of view that you both do not share. So I'll not get in the middle of this as long as my needs are fulfilled. If you find yourself in a position to fulfill your duty, I'll not interfere. May I eat now?" Apperson entered the main tent and sat at a table.

Cole suppressed the smile creeping across his face and followed the major into the tent.

"I can't believe your indifference to my authority!" Perry shouted.

"Believe it, sir. Would you be so good as to pass me the jam?"

When Perry refused the request, Cole was eager to retrieve the small jar for his new benefactor. "There's another thing I need to tell you," he said to Apperson. "And I have to say we may have to turn back."

Apperson stopped in mid bite of his eggs and looked up at Cole. "Are you mad? What now?" Dr. Reeves entered the tent and Cole took a deep breath to continue.

"We met up with a Texas Ranger yesterday. He's hunting a bunch of Comanches he says killed some settlers and burnt down their houses. He was heading in the same direction after them that we're looking to go."

With raised eyebrows Apperson took the bite and swallowed. "I wish the man luck. Why does this trouble you?"

Now Cole was bewildered. "It troubles me due to the fact they're Comanches. Indians don't come no worse than them."

"Really?" Apperson grinned first to Cole, then Perry, and finally to the woman. He took another bite. "I see no reason for worry, Mr. Cole. I have complete faith in your ability to protect us. Is anyone going to eat besides me?"

"You ain't listening. We've got to turn back. That ranger only took three tin horns and I could tell by the way he talked he wasn't looking forward to meeting up with that bunch. We wouldn't have a chance against them leading two women and, with due respect, two old men."

"I regret to agree," Perry said, staring at Cole, then looking to the Englishman. "Chasing hostiles into their own territory, where they know the lay of the land, it might take a division of trained soldiers to snuff them out."

"Rubbish!" Apperson dabbed jam on a biscuit. "We'll pay them for passage. We'll reason with them. We'll bargain."

Cole let out a long breath. He glanced at the woman, unsure whether to share his thoughts, but the truth could sway her from wanting to go on. "They won't bargain. They'll see a small party, carrying food, water, and a white woman with red hair. They'll want her and the Mexican girl too. After they're through killing all the men, if they don't keep both of them for themselves, they'll sell the doctor to slave traders in Mexico for guns and supplies." He hesitated. "Once they're done with her."

"Don't try to frighten me, Mr. Cole. I'm not afraid," she said.

Both Perry and Cole looked at her with surprise. "You need to be," said Cole. "There's a Comanche chief named Quanah Parker. His mother was a white woman that got took on a raid when she was a girl." He paused to let his temper settle. "When I first heard of pony tracks around here, I thought they might be Apache from New Mexico. They normally just steal what they need and run off in the night. But Comanches, they take it personal that you strayed into their territory. And they'll hunt you down, night or day, take what they can use and set fire to what they don't, including people. Once I heard it was Comanches, I knew why they weren't Apaches in these parts. The ones that didn't know better to leave are dead."

Apperson placed his fork on his plate and dabbed his lips with a napkin. "Oh come now," he said, "I'm not a novice when dealing with the local natives. There was another sort I encountered when I was in Africa in July of '79. The Zulu had been in the region for hundreds of years. There were literally thousands of them, all attired in their beads and hides to intimidate us, carrying spears, which they were quite adept at hurling at considerable distances. They routed Her Majesty's troops so badly we thought for a time it would be we who would have to withdraw. But once they were shown our proper resolve not to yield and they tasted the fire from our guns, it was they who withdrew and we were only a force of a few hundred."

Cole stared him in the eye. "Did that tribe have horses and know the use of repeating rifles?" The question brought a shroud of silence in the tent.

"Excuse me, sir," Jeffers said from the opening. "The Belgian gentleman is approaching."

A broad smile came over Apperson's face. "How wonderful!" He rose from his chair and quickly walked outside with Cole and the others behind. A single rider on a buckskin horse came from the east and reined in at the middle of the camp. He too had a wide smile as Apperson offered a handshake. The rider was wearing a dark brown hat with one side of the brim pinned to the crown, light green coat and pants garnished with a black belt and sash, and riding boots. He dismounted and briskly accepted Apperson's hand. After mutual slaps to the shoulder, the Englishman escorted his new guest in front of the others. "May I introduce you all to Monsieur Serge Mouton. He has agreed to join us on our journey."

Mouton first went to Dr. Reeves and when she offered a handshake, he removed his hat and pecked the back of her hand. He then offered his hand to Perry and Cole, who accepted it, although not sure what to make of this foreigner.

"I am pleased to meet you-all," he said with a peculiar accent Cole had not heard before.

"Is it just you or did you bring the rest of your army?" Perry said.

Mouton chuckled at the remark and shook his finger in the air. "No, I am by myself. However, I have what may take the place of all armies." He went to his horse and unbuttoned a scabbard to draw a carbine rifle of unusual design. Polished red wood encased the bluish-black metal to the first quarter of the barrel. At the midpoint a weaved pattern was cut into a separate piece of wood of which a long rod extended from it to the lock. A horizontal bolt and slot cut to the size of long round were on the right side of the firing mechanism. As he turned the weapon, a gaping hole was easily noticeable at the bottom. "This is all I need bring with me."

"Yes, you see, Mouton here is an inventor. This rifle is his own product. When we met in San Antonio I convinced him to test it on some of these natives that you so fear we may encounter."

"That is true," Mouton added. "I am hoping to demonstrate it to your army," he said to

Perry. "But they refuse to allow me to. So, I am here, and when they learn of its efficiency against the Indians that you battle, I am sure they will want to supply all of the soldiers with it." He offered it to the major to inspect.

"How many did you bring with you?" asked Cole.

"Just this one. This is the original, which I use myself. I cannot afford to bring the rest to this country without assurances from your army."

"One?" Cole scoffed. "That ain't going to do us no good."

With the same smile that never really left his face, Mouton politely took the rifle from Perry while looking at Cole. "Let me demonstrate." He went back to the buckskin and pulled off a small pouch, which he looped around his neck. A moment later he took a carton as big as his palm and inserted it into the bottom of the rifle by pulling back the bolt and locking it forward. A firm grasp of the wood grip let him pump the action. "Do you see that flower?" he said as he aimed the rifle. In an instant he fired and a boom louder than any Winchester rippled the air.

Cole barely had time to notice the yellow yucca blooms puff about and scatter in the light breeze. "Damn good shot."

"I'll say," added Perry. "I'd judge those at more than fifty yards.

The proud Mouton nodded. "A range up to fifteen hundred meters. A seven millimeter rifle cartridge. A true rifle cartridge. Armed with this weapon, a soldier can kill or wound his enemy to end all fighting. Your Samuel Colt says his pistol is the Peacemaker. This weapon that I hold is the savior of mankind."

Apperson smirked and slapped Mouton's back. "Undoubtedly, sir. May I offer you refreshment after your long trip?" The two men walked toward the tent.

"How can a thing made to kill people be thought a savior of men?" Cole asked as he and Perry followed.

"It alone can end warfare throughout the world. With its accuracy and ability to fire rapidly, no enemy would dare charge against it."

"A great miscalculation, sir." Perry said. "That claim has been made before." All of them stopped to face each other. "Dr. Gatling held the same idea. He was sure that his weapon would be the answer to ending war due to its rapid fire, and it shoots a .50 caliber bullet. I assure you, although it has proved useful in the field, it has not ended the fighting in the West." He shook his head. "A weapon so terrible it would end all wars? Inconceivable."

Now Mouton's smile turned to a confident grin. "That is because it is an artillery gun, not a combat weapon for every soldier. I have seen this gun of which you speak." He removed the carton from the rifle. "You see how easily loaded this weapon can be."

"Yeah, but how many bullets can you put in that thing?"

"The magazine holds nine." He opened the flap of the pouch. "But you see I keep six more magazines here. The Springfield rifle must be reloaded after each shot. The Winchester can hold fifteen bullets but once empty, it must be reloaded one bullet at a time. Mine can be reloaded in just seconds. That is why it is so unmatchable. That is why once I get your country to patent my rifle, all other weapons, including those of Winchester and Gatling, will never be used again."

Apperson's admiration for his new friend was clear when he wrapped his arm around Mouton's shoulder.

Cole stared at Perry propped against a wagon wheel amid the campfire's glow. He hadn't any sleep for nearly two days, due to this one man. With a bowl of the night's meal in his right hand, he knelt next to the major, who eyed his every move. The others were still in the main tent and out of earshot of any noise. Cole drew the bowie knife. The blade shined like a star. Although he knew it could put a quicker end to his troubles, he decided on another strategy, which would allow him sleep for the rest of his life. Without a word, he slipped it behind Perry's back, and sliced through the rope that bound the major's hands.

Perry wearily shook the blood back into his arms and accepted the bowl. "I don't suppose you laced this with poison."

"I wouldn't have to if you knew what was in it. It's some kind of soup. It tastes awful. But it won't kill you."

Perry sniffed at the bowl and gripped the

spoon. "I'm surprised. I would think you'd like to have me dead."

"I told you before, if I wanted, I'd have put a bullet through your heart when I had the chance."

"Likewise." Perry slurped the soup and cringed. "You're right. This is awful." The reaction made Cole smirk, but the matter he'd come to settle was still in mind.

"I guess you're right. There have been times when you got the drop on me. How come you didn't just shoot me?"

"Because that wouldn't have resolved the matter." Perry took another slurp from the spoon. Another pained gag led him to splash the dust with the remainder in the bowl. "I'd rather starve."

"You mean you killing me wouldn't make you a hero?"

"That's exactly it. You're a criminal, Clay. Your flight from justice has made you one. But even criminals deserve a trial. If I'd brought you back to Fort Lincoln across a saddle, then I'd be the one accused of murder. I don't relish a court martial any more than you do." He dipped his head to the ground, then back at Cole. "But I'll do it, if I must."

Both men looked each other in the eye.

"I ain't going back. Across a saddle or any other way."

"No," Perry chuckled. "You'll probably end up dead and scalped along with these other fools. What is it these people are here for?"

Shaking his head, Cole looked to the ground.

"I can't say I understand exactly what it is, but they're looking for some lost treasure some tribe from Mexico hid up around here somewhere a long time back."

"Aztec treasure? That's a myth. They can't be out here looking for that!"

"That they are," Cole said.

"Then you're a bigger fool then I thought you to be if you agreed to stay with them. You heard what the ranger said. Those hostiles will wipe out every one of you. You said it yourself."

"I know," said Cole, looking to the stars. "But something tells me I need to stay."

"You can't be serious. Suppose you aren't killed by the savages, you'll run out of water while traveling in circles, looking for this ridiculous treasure." The major held a tone of reason which Cole almost confused with a friend's warning.

"What would I have to lose? It ain't as if you're offering anything better."

The words cut into Perry. Even through the officer's bushy beard, Cole could see drawn cheeks. "I'm offering you a chance to clear your name. To come back to civilization and stand against the charges of treason. I'm offering you your honor."

"Damn bit a good that'll do me. I'd be lucky if you didn't call out the command to fire."

"There was a time I might have volunteered to do just that. But things have changed."

Cole's head jerked around at the officer. Any slack in Miles Perry's determination to bring back a traitor in chains was more of a surprise

71

than had it started snowing at that moment. "What's changed? You told me you still wanted me to go back with you."

"Yes." Perry nodded. "I do. But since I've been on your trail these last years, there has been an investigation into the massacre at the Little Big Horn. I read about it in the newspapers. It seems that sniveling weasel of a soldier Reno, together with that slouch Benteen, have testified against the wisdom of Custer's orders. The army wanted to know why they didn't support Custer's flank when he charged. They blamed overwhelming opposition and said they couldn't hear the shots coming from over the hill." He gritted his teeth. "I heard them. I heard the shots. We could have supported Custer, but Reno ordered us to dig in, even after the pressure had eased. Those cowards! I told them we could advance, but I was told to hold my position. And so, like a soldier, I obeyed my orders and the greatest general the army has known since Washington and five companies were slaughtered like cattle. I know, I was there."

"So was I, Major," said Cole in a cold, stern voice. "I don't know what was said at no trial, but there ain't no way no how that you could have saved Custer. He was swarmed on like bees do a hive. He was a fool for charging down that hill, Miles. I saw it with my own eyes."

Perry's lips showed the friendly part of the conversation was over. "Yes, don't I know.

That's why we are both here. Bonded by the same nightmare, only on different sides."

"So then nothing has changed?"

"What's changed is my purpose for taking you back to Fort Lincoln. To settle the record as you stated back on the ridge in Colorado. The story that you were sent to warn the Sioux of our advance on the orders of President U.S. Grant."

"I wasn't sent to warn nobody!" Cole shouted. "He sent me to try and talk Sitting Bull back to the reservation, to accept the terms that Red Cloud did. To try to stop the bloodshed that there turned out to be. Only your 'boy general' couldn't hear his own Indian scouts telling him two thousand Lakota painted for war were waiting on him over the brass bands playing in his ears parading him back to Washington and into the president's chair."

Before the officer blurted a reply, he bit his lip. "Fine, so be it. We've had this discussion before. Let's come to the agreement that we'll not convince each other to our different views. All I want is you to tell your story before a military court. Come back with me, Cole. Clear your name."

The offer took root in Cole's ears. Five years dodging the law had worn into him enough he didn't close his mind to ideas of standing before generals to tell the tale he knew as the truth and being able to ride free into any town. The truth had a price. "I would if I could. But I can't. If I was to tell what I knew, it would take Grant down. The man is like a father to me after my own got killed in the war. I swore I'd never do that."

"What kind of father would want a son to bear his burden?" Perry said in a consoling whisper. "Did he ask you to hide the truth on his behalf?"

Cole looked to the ground. "No. I just took it on my own that it was the proper thing to do."

"Then, perhaps you should come to Washington and ask him. I can't say I think much of the man, but I know him to be a honorable soldier. He hasn't been president for four years. There's no harm you can cause him. It seems he would want you to do the proper thing for yourself."

Cole kept his eyes on the dirt. All the years of holding to the notion of sacrificing his own happiness for a beloved mentor began to ease from his shoulders. Maybe it was time to allow himself the peace he had searched for on the run, and it took the man chasing him all those years to plant that seed with words instead of a gun. He faced Perry.

"I'll think about it. But I can't leave these folks."

"Come to your senses. You can't go with these people. It's suicide. You've done all you can. You warned them and shouldn't harbor any guilt as to what happens to them."

"That's just it," said Cole. "I do care what happens to them. Hell, I know it's crazy. But they haven't a chance out there on their own."

He paused, recalling Jane Reeves's face against the breaking dawn. She held that wondering smile, showing her belief in going after what she wanted. "I gave them my word."

"Then I'll come with you."

A clap of thunder wouldn't have startled Cole more. "Like hell you are."

"If you plan to go through with this absurd idea, then you'll need all the help you can get."

"To be any good, you'd have to carry a gun. With you looking at my back?" Cole shook his head. "I don't need that kind of help, thank you."

The major let out a long breath. "I give my word as an officer, so long as I have yours, that I will help you and this party until we can go no farther. I don't expect that to be very long."

Cole continued to peer in the soldier's eyes, unsure of what trick to expect, but the voice he heard sounded sincere. "Why would you want to do that?"

Perry slumped his head, showing the crown of the dusty blue hat with crossed swords. "Because I don't have anywhere else to go."

"What are you talking about?"

"Just what I said." Perry looked at Cole. "I've been tracking you since I heard you were in Colorado. That was almost two years ago. I allowed my zeal to catch you to cloud my judgement as an officer in the army. I'm absent from my command." His tone grew louder. "I thought it was my duty to capture a suspected traitor to the Seventh Cavalry, so I pursued you, and in so doing, now I am a wanted man."

With his head vacant for a reply, Cole warily

watched Perry as the major stood and looked at the sky.

"I've been in the army for eighteen years. I joined the Michigan Volunteers to be under the command of one of the best men I ever knew, General George A. Custer. Gettysburg is spoken of as a tragic battle, but it was a great day for me. With our losses, the general himself promoted me from lieutenant to captain. It was that day I knew I belonged in this capacity. When the war was over, I wanted to continue. So I joined him when he was assigned to the Seventh. I was never so proud. I was an officer. I held a command. I was a man." He looked to the side. "Until that day in Montana. Since then, I've never felt the same. There's always a shadow hanging over the unit. When I learned you were within my grasp, the same pride that filled me before returned. I've been following you since, in the belief I could regain the dignity it meant to be in the Seventh Calvary. Now, I've neglected my duty. My last dispatch ordered me to report to Fort Davis for what I'm sure is a court-martial." He looked at Cole. "That is why I'm willing to help you. Because without you, my life, the life I've known and cherished, is over."

Cole rose, trying to decide whether to accept the offer. It would be foolish, but a feeling returned to him as well. A feeling that he could sense the truth in what he was being told. He too had something taken from him on that day Custer died. Holding out his hand to the major, he agreed to begin the end of the torment that bonded both of them. "All right, Miles. I used to know what it meant for a soldier to give his word. So I'll give you mine. We get these folks what they want, and then I'll go back with you and get this over with."

Perry took Cole's hand. "You have my word."

Chapter Six

The call to rise came with the rattle of pots, pans and any other object Cole could find to make noise. His warning the night before to strike camp early had fallen on less than sober ears. The racket was the only way he knew to pierce the fog that clogged them. Dawn would break in an hour and the best time of day to start traveling was quickly passing.

First to poke her head from a tent was Dr. Reeves. The fire lit her face as red as her hair. Likely it matched her mood; which appeared part sleepy, part confused and the rest irritated. Jeffers was quick to run from his tent, slipping on his dust stained white coat to hurry into the tent of his boss.

A peek behind showed a rising Major Perry. Cole reached for the unloaded Schofield tucked into his belt. The idea of returning it wasn't yet a comfort to him.

More banging of metal increased the step of everyone.

"Please, stop that infernal noise," came a cry from Apperson's tent. An instant later, the gentleman stuck his head from the canvas flap.

"We need to load these tents and be moving by sunup."

"But, Mr. Cole, I daresay it won't allow us time to finish breakfast before then."

"You got that right, Mr. Apperson. We'll be eating during the ride. Best tell your cook to find last night's meal and wrap a biscuit around it. We'll need to be moving near five miles before midday. I figure the heat will take most of your strength by then. But I want to be at that water hole by sundown."

"Good heavens, man. No breakfast! That's outrageous." Apperson gave him a congenial smile like a father to a child. "Come back here in an hour or so, and we'll have another look at the day's plan at that time."

"Not if you want me to lead this outfit." Cole's firm tone soured the smile into a reluctant nod of compliance.

Apperson paused and drew a long breath. "Very well, then," he muttered.

For the next hour, Cole acted as a sergeant over his troops, peppering everyone with orders. The women had left their tent, allowing Cole to bundle the canvas and poles into the large wagon with help from Jeffers.

Apperson, too, relinquished his shelter,

although not with the same speed as the others. He drank from a cup. Cole caught a whiff of what he thought was liquor and his puzzled face produced a sly smile from the Englishman.

"Brandy. It takes the chill from the bones."

While Cole pulled stakes, a framed image on a wooden stand caught his eye. It was a photograph of Apperson wearing a hat shaped like a bowl, with rifle in hand, kneeling next to an animal the same bulk as a longhorn steer. Its hide was bare of hair, the ears were twice the size of any cow, and two unmatched horns jutted from its snout. Although upright, it appeared to be laid atop all fours and shot dead, judging by the gentleman's calm pose.

Cole squinted at the picture. "What the hell is that?"

"Oh," replied Apperson in a proud voice. "That's my most prized trophy to date. Mustn't leave this behind." He tucked the frame under his arm, until he noticed Cole's interest. Then he displayed it with both hands.

"A rhinoceros, Mr. Cole. Magnificent beast, although a bit of a foul temper, to be sure. I was on holiday in Africa some years past. While on safari, we were walking through the bush stalking lion when we happened upon this fellow. Most of the wildlife would flee at the snap of a twig, but not this one. Firm he stood, smelling the air. They have an acute sense of smell, but they're near blind as a mole. Once it was clear he caught my scent, I knew he would come at me. And so he did, lowering the head and charging, first at a trot and quickly at full speed."

"Did you climb the nearest tree?" Cole asked with a matter of fact tone.

"Good heavens, no. I held my ground and carefully aimed my rifle." He winked with a gleaming smile. "My gun misfired. A moment from death, I pulled the bolt back, ejecting the shell, reloaded and pointed the muzzle right in line with that massive horn and fired." Apperson tapped the frame glass. "I brought him down with that shot, right in his tracks. Quite a close call, that was. It was him or me, I was nearly killed." He looked at Cole with somber eyes. "Odd feeling one gets when he faces death. I never felt more alive."

After a moment, the Englishman grinned and nodded. "Carry on, Mr. Cole. We shouldn't waste the day talking about the past."

With the wagon loaded, the sun had already crept into the sky. Cole scanned the clear horizon then peeked at the party. Apperson was settling into his seat next to Jeffers, while Jane Reeves and Adela with her baby found spots among the cargo in the back. The small cart was firmly harnessed to the rear with the burro tethered to follow. Mouton as well as Major Perry were mounted and flanked the wagon. Cole whistled and pointed to the west. "Let's move out."

By the time the sun was directly overhead, they had made close to four miles. Cole rode to a rise to survey what lay ahead. Sandstone hills

Tim McGuire

of brown and red extended out from the rolling white sand dotted with scrub and sage. He peered back at the wagon. A four horse team required a sizable amount of water. Not having traveled as far as he wanted and with a steep landscape yet to cross, he resigned himself to the fact that to maintain even a slow pace, a rest was needed for the animals' sake.

Riding back, he reined in to parallel the wagon. "We'll pull up at the base of those rocks up ahead and water the horses. If you want to eat, do it in the meantime, but we won't light no fires. No telling how far it'll travel or who could see it. I don't want to be sitting long."

"Very well," said Apperson. "How far do you estimate to the water hole you mentioned?"

Cole shook his head. "I can't rightly know till we pass the next row of hills." About to spur his horse to tell the others, Cole was stopped with Apperson's blurted call.

"Oh, Mr. Cole. There is a matter I've been meaning to address. This fellow you've brought along, your friend the major."

"He ain't my friend."

"Nevertheless, he's here as part of your circumstances. Not of mine. I hope there should be no trouble between you two. We can't have distractions. Don't misunderstand, if the issue is settled between you and he, I don't object to his being with us. So long as he can trusted to keep our purposes confidential. However, there is the matter of payment. My offer was to you. I wasn't anticipating further expenses, if you know what I mean."

Cole cracked a grin. "If you're worried about paying him, I can tell you now he ain't here for the money. He's here for something else. Leave it at that."

Apperson nodded. "Very well, I shall. And the condition of confidentiality? You'll accept accountability?"

"I can vouch for him, if that's what you're asking. He thinks this is a damn fool mistake as it is."

"How splendid," the Englishman said with a bob of the head. "I'll leave you to your duties, Mr. Cole."

Puzzled by Apperson's manner, Cole reined the palomino around to catch up with Perry but was quickly approached by Mouton.

"It is it very much longer?"

Pointing a finger, Cole answered, "I just told them that we'll stop to water the stock at the base of them rocks."

"Good. It will give me a chance to see more of the land."

"We won't be stopping that long," Cole said, shaking his head. "It's hard enough to keep going while you're moving. I'd just as soon keep the time we're stopped as short as I can."

Mouton swiped his brow of sweat. "We will not camp?"

"Nope. As slow as we're going, It'll be a good take just to get to the water before night falls. If we ain't there, it's hard to find something in the black of night."

"Perhaps next time when you go out, I can come, yes?"

The idea didn't appeal to Cole. Parading foreigners to see the sights in hostile land wasn't high on his mind at the time. "Today wouldn't be a good idea. I'll let you know when it's better."

Before Mouton could prepare a plea, Cole spurred his horse and rode next to Perry, then reined in.

"How much further to the water?" asked Perry.

"We'll rest the horses at the foot of those hills."

"We're pressing on after that, I hope," the officer said with a questioning stare.

"That we are."

The answer was met with an approving nod from Perry. "I should guess we'll reach the water by sundown."

"That we will. I don't care to be moving at night."

With all expectations satisfied, Perry slackened his commanding scowl. "You know I still think this mission a folly. If it weren't for my situation, I could ride to Fort Concho or Fort Stockton and get a trooper escort all the way into Mexico."

"Well," Cole snickered, "I told Apperson you had that mind toward this. But he don't want nobody knowing why he's out here. I guess he's rattled about somebody finding what he's looking for first."

Perry leaned closer. "This is insane, Cole. You know it. Once we're camped near water, you will have given them a fair chance to make

it to civilization from there. Why not abandon
this foolishness and we can be on our way?"

"I said I'd given them my word," Cole sternly
replied. "The same one I gave you." Irritated by
the proposal, he pulled away from the disgusted major and ambled back to the wagon.
The two old men were still on the seat, and
Adela's arm was curled around a blanket,
which no doubt cradled her child. The absence
of the woman doctor made him circle to the
other side. There, wearing a broad-brimmed
Panama hat of straw, walked Dr. Reeves.

"If you're going ask me about the water," he
said slowing the palomino to walk next to her,
"we should be there by day's end."

She squinted up at him. "I wasn't going to
ask. It is what you said at the camp before we
left."

Recalling what she said was true and feeling
a fool for it, he thought to change the mood.
"You often walk in the desert, or did you just
feel a need to ease the weight on the team?"
His remark was meant to poke fun, but her
curled lip short of a sneer made him feel a
greater fool.

"I do often walk, Mr. Cole. It's good for the
blood." She kept her eyes to the front. Uneasy
with her tone and in attempt to make amends for
his jest, he dismounted and walked beside her.

"If I said something you took offense to, like
you being too much weight for the horses, like
that, I was only fooling. It ain't that you look
that heavy."

85

She shot him a wide-eyed glare, which, had it been a punch, would have put him on the dirt, then she quickly pointed her nose straight ahead.

"I didn't mean like that, as in heavy." As he fumbled in his mind for the right words, she freed him from the burden.

"I understood what you meant, Mr. Cole." She faced him and said in a snide voice, "That is your name today, isn't it?" She snapped her face again to the front.

Although her temper was made clear, he was relieved to know what bothered her. "Oh, that's it. I thought I told you the reason for that back at the camp too."

"Perhaps to your satisfaction, but not to mine. I was always taught a lie was a poor way to begin a conversation when meeting someone for the first time."

"Yes, ma'am. So was I. But there are times when it's best for those concerned."

"For my benefit, or for yours?" She looked at him. "Is what Major Perry accused you of true?"

Not wanting to open that powder keg, he looked away a moment and scratched his chin. "There ain't a quick answer to that. But I can say that him and me don't see eye to eye on that or a lot of the same things."

By her marched stride next to the wagon, he could tell he hadn't budged her mind a bit about him.

"You remember the first night in the camp, you talked about that woman who followed this Cortés fellow and helped him? You said she was thought a traitor for doing it."

"That's not the same. She loved him. He was the father of her child. Besides, she was only called that by her enemies."

"Well..." He paused a moment trying to compare his own situation. "You could say about the same thing with me. The army ain't really my enemy, but they don't know the whole story." He took a long breath. "I did what I did for reasons nobody but me and another man knows. But after I'm done with what I told you folks I was going to do, me and the major are going to head out together to set things straight."

Her glance made him believe he succeeded, but the tone to her words convinced him otherwise. "And the name Hayes, did you take that off some bottle?"

"No," he answered, sensing his own tone becoming solemn. "That was given to me. I wouldn't have used it if I held no pride for it. A widow woman and her boy and girl took me in when I was in a bad way. It was their name, the name of her husband."

The clear image of the ten-year-old Noah Hayes and that of the young mother Ann flashed before him. Days spent on their farm, building a barn with the boy, the delight of settling in one place as part of a family, the remembrance of a woman's soft touch against his skin. The gunfight with a lawman and the escape on a stolen palomino to give the family peace from his troubles flushed away the vision.

"I guess it was wrong of me to use their name," he said while coming out of his daydream. "I can't blame you for thinking bad of mine, but I wouldn't want you to hold the same against theirs." He peeked at her to see a glimmer of a smile on her face. "Anyways, those that have been my friends call me Clay."

Her smile widened. "And mine call me Jane."

Chapter Seven

Cole came upon the water hole and was relieved to see the level had changed little in two days. He climbed off the palomino and splashed his face. Wiping his eyes of the afternoon heat and scooping a quick drink, he judged the party about two hours behind. A glimpse at the sun revealed enough light left in the day for their arrival near sundown. The decision to scout ahead, even though cautious, had resulted in little to be concerned about. Despite what he first thought with the late start, all appeared to be going according to plan.

A booming blast rippled the silence, echoing from the south, then east and north, passing over him like a wave in a river. Cole rose and scanned the horizon for any signs of the shooter, but only the scrub was on the basin.

Two more shots erupted, with the same confusion as to their direction. Fearful the party was being fired upon, he mounted the palomino and spurred its flanks to gallop back to the wagon.

Lather on the horse had him rein in to an amble. He was unsure of the palomino's limit and it was no time to find himself afoot. Once over a small rise, he saw the party close by. Upon approach of the wagon, Major Perry rode out to meet him.

"Everybody all right?" asked Cole.

Perry nodded. "So far. We heard shots. Sounded like rifle fire."

"Yeah, I couldn't tell where they came from." Both riders ambled their mounts to join the others. Apperson and Jeffers sat in the box with both women poking their heads out from the canvas. "You folks okay?"

Jeffers pulled up the horses. Apperson nodded and said, "Very well, Mr. Cole. What was all that gunfire about?"

"Can't say," Cole answered, dismounting and cupping water from his canteen under his horse's nose while peeking around the wagon. "Where's that fellow Mouton?"

"He rode off when we stopped to rest the horses," Perry said. Cole gave a look of shock and Perry nodded in agreement. "I tried to talk him out of it, but he had his mind made up."

"He said he asked you if he could come along," Jane Reeves added.

"Did he tell you I told him no?"

"Yes," she said with a nod. "I believe that was

part of the reason he left while you were gone. He said he wanted to see more of the land and would meet us at the water hole."

Cole looked at Perry, who also thought the mention peculiar. "How does he know where it is?"

"I can't answer that," she said, then Apperson raised his finger.

"Obviously, confidence in his ability as a reconnaissance soldier, no doubt."

"He is a soldier?" asked a surprised Perry.

"Yes, I thought I mentioned it." Apperson chuckled. "The memory slipping, the first signs of senility, they say."

"What kind of soldier? For who?"

"Well," Apperson said, appearing confused, "if I recall correctly, I think he said it was for the French. Something about him serving with their army to force the Dutch from Belgium. He told me that when I met him near the Congo River."

"Then, why is he here?" asked Perry.

"Discharged, I'm sure. That was more than fifteen years ago, Major. We can't expect everyone to serve their entire life, now can we?"

Perry showed disdain for the remark. "Some of us have a greater sense of duty." He looked to Cole, who met his gaze.

"Yeah," said Cole, stepping into the stirrup, turning to Apperson. "Well, what if he met up with them Comanches?"

"An unfortunate possibility, I agree. Perhaps you should have a look for him, Mr. Cole?"

Cole closed his eyes for a moment. "I figured you were going to say that."

"I'm sure he hasn't wandered too far. A man of your experience should be able to find him without much time spent, I'd say." Apperson pointed to Perry. "We'll rely on the good auspices of Major Perry to lead us the rest of the way."

Cole faced the major and took a long breath. "I guess if I leave him out there to get scalped that would be another thing you'd hold against me."

"No," Perry said. "I could look the other way. I really don't care for the man. But I agree something must be done. He's been out there for nearly two hours, and if he doesn't find the water, I don't give much for his chances."

With a single nod, Cole reined the palomino around. About to kick the flanks, he stopped and held the reins firm, feeling the major's eyes locked at his belt. Cole drew the Schofield, and stared at it. He was still not comfortable with arming the man who had once held him at gunpoint, but the time had come for him to live up to what he agreed to and to earn and test Perry's trust.

"I guess you'll have need of this," he said, handing the pistol to Perry. Cole popped six cartridges from his gunbelt and dropped them into the major's hand. The two men shared a moment of mutual faith. "I'll be back by sundown or near after." He glanced at the wagon. "Tell them to cook something worth eating."

Perry smiled and Cole rode away.

With his rifle firmly pointed before him, Mouton stealthily approached the fire lighting up the night. As he came through the brush, three men in sombreros and bandoliers crouched around the flame in conversation. While their pistols were still holstered, he took a long breath and came into the light. They were startled by his presence and quickly drew their weapons, but couldn't bring them above the waist, stopped by the rifle steadied at them.

Mouton bobbed his head for them to throw the guns to the dirt, and after a glance at one another, they did so. He waved the rifle barrel for them to raise their hands. As six arms went into the air, Mouton carefully stepped to where one pistol lay and slowly bent to pick it up. As he squatted, the ratchet of a hammer being cocked froze him.

The sound came from behind, but he dared not turn. He felt a muzzle at his back, then a hand reached around him to grip the rifle and pull it from his grasp.

The hatless leader came into view in front. He had dark black hair but lighter skin than his friends. Holding the rifle in one hand, he pointed a revolver at Mouton's chest with the other. Admiring the unique weapon, he smiled, raising his head to Mouton, who looked him in the eye and didn't know if he had guessed right or would be shot dead on the spot. The others retrieved their guns.

"You are late, señor."

Mouton let out a long held breath. He had guessed right. "It is a long way. I had to find my way mostly in the dark and did not know if I had come to the right people. I see your English of the Americans is better than my Spanish."

"We were ready to leave, but as I see, I am happy we did not."

"I knew you would think that way," Mouton said. "It is the finest in the world, yes?"

"So you said before." The leader sniffed at the rifle's muzzle. "You had trouble?"

Mouton nodded. "Three men that were behind me. I could not be certain if they would follow, so I had to make it certain that they would not," he said as he watched the rifle passed to the other men. Grunted laughter showed their admiration of the weapon.

"Did you know who they were?" asked the leader.

"No." Mouton shook his head. "I am sure they were not your men. They seem to be Americans, but they were so far away, I did not know who they might be."

The leader showed his appreciation for Mouton's caution. "It is best to be careful. Come. Share our food. Let us talk of the delivery of the other rifles."

"The rifles will be here soon by train, which you will have to thieve. I appreciate your hospitality, but I must refuse. I have been gone too long from my friends. I think they might start to look for me."

With a more solemn face, the leader looked to the ground. "My men tell me that the woman is still with them."

"*Oui*. She is."

"I heard also there are more men with them now. Who are they?"

"An American soldier," said Mouton, removing his hat and wiping his brow. "A major. I do not know his capacity, but it seems he is without soldiers to command. And there is another man. He is quite different. A man of large height, he appears one used to combat. A good fighter. We must keep him in our view all the time."

"And the name of this man?"

"Cole, a Mr. Clay Cole."

"I do not know of him. But no matter, he will die too if necessary. I will have my son back." The leader took the rifle away from its careless use by the others and reprimanded them. "This is a fine weapon, *mi amigo*. If it will do all that you say, then we will be successful in killing the men of Diaz and ending the tyranny like that of the days of Santa Anna."

"And you still control those raiders?" asked Mouton.

"*Los indios* seek the same as us. To rule their own land. They will use your rifles to keep *los diablos Tejanos* from interfering."

Mouton took the rifle with a wide smile. "You are a man of great vision, *monsieur*. Together, we will bring a change to Mexico. You will rule the north, while the same revolution will restore the order of those I serve." Mouton turned to enter the surrounding brush.

"Do they still search for *El Dorado*?"

The question stopped Mouton, who faced his friend with another wide smile. "*Oui*. The pitiful dream of the Englishman. We will turn it to our advantage." He entered the brush.

"A-dieu."

* * *

The fire climbed higher, fueled by dry scrub. A rustle from behind brought Jeffers quickly to his feet to assist Adela with the bucket of drawn water. Apperson leaned closer to the fire to take a flamed stick to ignite his cigar. Once it was lit, he reclined in his wooden folding chair, exhaling a long plume.

"A good day's travel, I'd say."

"What I'd say is that we were fortunate to get to the water before sundown," said Perry, bringing more firewood.

"Forever the pessimist, eh, Major?"

"Not a pessimist, Mr. Apperson, a realist." He knelt next to the fire and tossed in a stick. "Without escort, every day that we can make camp and find water without loss of life is an extreme achievement."

Apperson seemed amused. "Come now, Major Perry. If this was the debacle you think it is, what are your reasons for accompanying us?"

"My reasons," Perry sternly repeated, "are my own."

"You are here for him," Jane said as she took a seat on a decayed log. "You're here for Clay."

Keeping a firm eye at her, he jabbed another stick into the flame. "That is true, Miss Reeves."

She felt a smirk cross her face at the officer's address, a slight she'd known since graduation when she dared to enter into the realm of science, an occupation reserved for men. She left the correction to Apperson's chivalry.

"I believe the title of doctor is more appropriate, Major, lest we refer to you as Mr. Perry." He looked to her with fond eyes. "I, of course, address her by her first name with permission, because of her youth and my incurable paternal instincts."

She smiled at the Englishman, then back at Perry, who tipped his cap.

"My apologies, Doctor," he said with due respect. "I meant no offense."

"None taken, Major Perry. I can't say I particularly insist on the title. I take no offense being referred to as Miss Reeves, or Jane . . ." she hesitated, catching his eye. "Should you feel more comfortable with it."

"I think I should feel more comfortable with 'doctor,' Doctor."

"As you wish, Major," she said.

Jeffers came from Apperson's side. The older man's weathered red face seemed to have taken a toll on his strength by sign of a wheezed speech. "Would you like me to prepare the evening meal, sir?"

"That would be splendid, Jeffers," Apperson answered, oblivious of his butler's condition. "What's on the menu?"

"I'm afraid we're out of any fresh meat. I was unable to hunt for any game. We do have dried beef and still some flour. It won't be up to its usual standard."

"All part of the conditions, Jeffers. I trust in your ability as a chef. Whatever you prepare will suffice."

"Very good, sir," Jeffers said and he went to the wagon.

Jane watched the servant's strained gait. "Are you sure he's all right?" she whispered to Apperson.

"Jeffers? The old boy needs a good night's sleep, that's all. As do all of us."

"Don't be so sure," Perry added. "He isn't accustomed to this heat. A man of his age won't acclimate as easily." The major glanced at Jane, then at Apperson. "It's likely to affect all of our better judgments."

"Another discouragement?" said Apperson. "Mr. Cole told me of your disapproval. I wouldn't have thought you'd be quite so hostile." He took another long puff from the cigar. "You must broaden your view of things, Major. Believe in what others see as poppycock."

"What makes you believe that you'll find treasure?" He rose in disdain. "Do you have a map showing where it is?"

"What we have is the contents of a letter from Cortés himself describing its whereabouts," Jane retorted.

"Yes, in a scrambled mix of languages, I understand. With due respect, Doctor, I hardly think this fortune hunt wise on that flimsy foundation." Perry's heated words were insulting. However, Jane restrained her urge to answer fire with fire. Reason had always been a better tactic.

"Major Perry, your attitude toward our ideas is not unlike those of people who believed the secrets of ancient Egypt weren't possible or plausible to understand. Questions about the origins of the pyramids and other mysteries were meant to remain unknown. Until the forces of Napoleon discovered by accident the Rosetta Stone. It was a template to interpret the hieroglyphics. Now they're finding out secrets that have been buried for centuries."

"I know what it is, Doctor. I am a student of history, as well," answered Perry. He continued to feed the fire on the ground, while making it obvious the one inside him was ablaze. "What does a pure act of utter happenstance have to do with this operation? Do you suppose to suggest his letter is a parallel?"

"Perhaps," said Jane, to which Perry scoffed.

"Yes, we do," Apperson said. "I understand your reluctance to place faith in the idea. However, you must admit that many of the discoveries that we take for granted today were derived from pure acts of happenstance, wouldn't you say? Columbus was looking for a route to Asia, for heaven's sake. What more evidence do you require?" The Englishman chuckled a bit and took another puff.

"Evidence of what?"

A reflective mood came over Apperson's face. He straightened in his chair, holding the cigar like a maestro conducting a symphony. "Fate, old boy. It's fate. Impossible to draw a diagram of logic from it. Nevertheless, there are forces beyond the control of mankind that drive men to unlock the secrets of the past, to do great things. Of this I am certain." He leaned back in the chair with a contented smile, puffing on the cigar, which he abruptly removed to speak. "Do understand, I don't share every extreme notion.

There are colossal blunders of history as well. Take that damn Frenchman who proposes building a canal across the isthmus of Panama. That," he chuckled, "is a ludicrous ambition. I have been there. History will show it a mistake. It will never succeed, mark my words."

Perry slowly shook his head. "Colossal blunders? I have been there, too, I regret to say." He picked up another stick and placed it gently into the fire. "I'll say this, Mr. Apperson. I find myself connected to one of the worst in my country's history. I've only worsened it with my own 'ludicrous ambition.' I guess yours can't be any worse than mine." The major's somber face was clear. The discussion had brought a painful memory, one about which Jane wished to learn more.

"Excuse me, sir," Jeffers announced as he approached. "The lady Adela has prepared cakes of flat flour. I believe she intends to roll the dried beef inside them as a form of sandwich. I trust you approve?"

"How enlightening," Apperson said, clapping his hands. "A native delicacy. I look forward to it, Jeffers."

"Very good, sir. I believe they should be served within the hour."

"My God." Apperson pulled out his pocket watch. "I'm famished. I can hardly believe the hour is so late." He snapped the watch cover closed. "Where the devil is Mr. Cole?"

Straining to see the ground for any tracks in the moonless night, Cole became more convinced with each step of the palomino that any further search for Mouton was pointless. He reined in and turned around in the pitch-black that surrounded him. An even bigger chore would be finding his own way to the water hole.

The air was still. No rustle of any creature hunting or escaping broke the silence. The sky was barren of stars, no doubt hidden by clouds traveling through. That foreigner was on his own. It was time to turn back.

He reined the palomino around, only to pull up upon the murmured stir of laughter. A scan of the dark horizon showed no sign of its source. Another ripple came from where he had been headed. The noise became louder so he eased off the horse, tethered the reins to a small tree and drew his Colt.

He followed the sound, moving both left and right, stopping until the clamor was loud enough for him to center it. As he walked, the ground steepened. Soon, his left hand pawed the dirt to keep his balance. He was careful of his step so as not to sound his approach. Distinct voices could be heard out of the clutter, and Mex Spanish was the language spoken.

The increasing incline had him almost prone, so he crawled higher, sighting the silhouetted edge of a small ridge carved out of the dark by the light of a fire. About to peek over the side, he thought his hat might show him before he wanted to be noticed, so he took it off. Two men flanked the fire and two full bedrolls lay on the outer edge of the camp.

The jabber continued, and Cole turned to

where the hill's slope was less steep. He crept a step, until frozen by the firm clamp of a hand across his mouth and a locked grip on his gun hand. A heavy weight collapsed him to the dirt. In reflex, he reared back but stopped upon a hissed voice.

"Easy there, Mr. Cole. Stop making racket or they'll kill us both."

Cole nodded, despite the stiff hold against his mouth, which slowly loosened. He looked over his shoulder and recognized the illuminated face of the ranger Chet Burroughs.

"Sorry for having to do that, but I couldn't have you making a ruckus."

Still angered at the tactic, Cole could only agree with the reason. "Where's the rest of your men?"

Burroughs swallowed hard. "Dead. All of them, I'm sad to say. Got cut off their animals by someone in the rocks. Would have had me too, but I was off pissing in the brush." A hint of a grin broke his face. "First time the urge has ever served a useful purpose. Still, it didn't do them young'uns no good."

"Was it one of those down there?"

"Couldn't tell who was doing the shooting. Hell, one of the slugs cut through one of them men and plugged my mount. A hell of a shot. I've been tracking where I saw the gunsmoke, keeping my distance so as not to draw further fire. Got here just as one of the gang was leaving. I haven't seen him come back yet."

Cole looked at the men again. "Well, whoever

they are, by the sign of them cartridge belts they're carrying, I'd say they ain't farmers."

"Not likely. That one closest to the fire without his hat, I seen him before. That's Francisco Gura. He's a Mexican rebel, was throwed in jail some months back for trying to build an army to take hold of Coahuila and make it his own. I heard they shot him."

"Looks like they missed."

"Just the same, you can bet he's on the run and will take anything he can get. Can you tell what they're saying? My hearing ain't that good."

"Ordering *cervezas* is my limit of the lingo." Cole scanned about. "You said one of them rode off?"

"Yup. Some time back. It was too dark to get a good look at him or where he was heading."

"The smart thing to do is leave," Cole said as he retrieved his hat. "No sense in swatting at a hornet's nest."

"Sounds good to me." Burroughs and Cole crawled on elbows and knees down the hill. "You still leading that party of Eastern folk?"

"I can't get them to turn back."

"Once they hear of this, it shouldn't be hard to convince them."

The sound of a rider approaching made Jane put down her plate and turn in the direction. Out of the corner of her eye, she could see Major Perry had a pistol drawn and waved to her to take cover. She quickly crouched behind the small log.

"Who goes there?" the major called.

"It's Cole and I'm bringing in the ranger," was the shouted reply.

Jane rose and watched Cole emerge from the dark and ride into the center of the camp. Apperson and Jeffers came from the tent. Adela came from Jane's tent with her child in her arms.

An old man with brown striped pants and coat climbed off the back of the palomino. Cole quickly dismounted and reined his horse to the brush.

"And who might this be?" asked Apperson.

"Chet Burroughs is my name. Captain in the Texas Rangers." Burroughs tipped his hat to Jane with a friendly face, which turned furrowed when he turned to the major. "What's he doing here?" Perry continued to point the pistol for a moment, then curled his lip as he holstered the weapon.

"I couldn't get him to leave, neither," Cole remarked.

"Is he still causing trouble for you?"

Cole took a long look at Perry, then dipped his eyes to the dirt. "We've come to an agreement."

"Good then. I'm too tired to put out any squabble between the two of you."

Apperson came to stand near the fire. "Where the devil have you been, Mr. Cole? I was beginning to think we might have to send Major Perry to search for you."

"I was doing what you asked me to do, looking for your friend Mutton."

"It is Mouton." The Belgian came from

behind Adela, holding his rifle, pointed at Cole and the ranger, but quickly he raised the muzzle to the air and showed his wide smile. "The 'n' is not said."

"Yes, well, he has been for some time now. Perhaps it would have been better judgment to send him after you?"

Apperson's remark showed on Cole. He stared at Mouton. "Where the hell were you?"

"I told you I wanted to see more of your beautiful Texas," said Mouton as he stepped around Adela. "I went and admired the wildflowers and tall mountains."

"They ain't *that* tall," said Cole. "Is that all you went for?"

"Why, yes, of course. Why do you ask?"

Burroughs pointed in the distance. "I lost three men out there. We were ambushed by a shooter in the rocks. Do you know anything about that?"

"Yes, of course we do," Apperson said. "We heard shots this afternoon."

"Oh, my dear." Jane covered her open mouth. "You were shot at?"

Burroughs nodded. "Yes, ma'am. We were. Three young men lay dead out there in the sand. And I was supposed to keep them from getting killed and I failed to do so. I'm feeling plumb sorry about that."

"How unfortunate," Apperson blurted. "You have my sympathies, Captain Burroughs. May we offer you some dinner?"

"I really don't feel like eating right now."

"I do," said Cole. Jeffers quickly went to the

back of the wagon and a plate of the dried beef tortillas was soon in Cole's hands. He took a seat on the log and Jane joined him.

"The thought of those men killed by the shots we heard. It makes one even sadder at the mention. Were you hurt, Captain Burroughs?"

"No, ma'am. I was off in the bush . . ." He hesitated. "I was looking for tracks."

A smirk came over Cole's face. "Was they wet?"

"No. They weren't," Burroughs sternly answered. "I don't think it's a matter to be laughing about." He looked at Jane. "I was off my horse, ma'am, when they were shot, cut right off their horses."

Jane put her head in her hands. The scene just described played in her mind. She had heard stories of violence in the West, but the idea of men murdered sank deep into her stomach.

"That ain't the worst of it," warned Cole as he bit the tortilla in two.

"Did you meet up with the renegades?" asked Perry.

With his mouth full, Cole mumbled while shaking his head. "Another bunch."

"What did you say? Speak clearly, man," Apperson demanded.

"What he's saying is that we spotted another bunch that's just as dangerous," Burroughs said. "Mexican rebels, headed up by a fellow named Francisco Gura."

A clanging echo made all eyes dart to a shocked Adela, who had dropped a tin cup. After a moment, she picked it up.

"Gura?" Perry said as if remembering the name. "There was a dispatch not long ago warning of his revolutionaries raiding across the border near El Paso."

"Well, it looks like they're trying their hand in these parts now." Burroughs accepted a cup of water from Jeffers. "Best thing for you folks to do is to follow me to the nearest town at first light."

"I'm afraid that's impossible, Captain. We're on an expedition here. We will not detour from my plans."

"Listen to the man," Perry pleaded to Apperson. "He just told you that not only are there renegades out there but now a Mexican rebel band that will attack us without mercy. They'll take our water, food and whatever they please. If for nothing else, our supplies are low. We should go to the nearest town or settlement to replenish the needs of your expedition."

Burroughs leaned closer to Cole. "He ain't as thickheaded as I thought. Even for a Yankee."

"He has a way of making sense. Like a woman, it kind of gnaws on a fellow." Cole turned to Apperson. "And much as it pains me to side with Major Perry, we need the shelter, and the horses need the rest and a few days graze while we still have the chance."

"I agree with Lord Apperson," said Mouton. "We should go on."

"With due respect," Perry snidely remarked, "you're a fool. I would think as a military man you should see the need for not extending a mission beyond its limit."

Mouton's eyes widened slightly, as if he were surprised by the major's discovery about his past.

"Yes," Apperson added. "I told them of your experience with the French." Mouton's eyes now narrowed at the Englishman. Jane sensed an uneasiness among all of the men. A compromise was needed from a woman's perspective.

"Lord Apperson, maybe we could seek a town. I for one could use the respite." She faced Adela. "This is no place for a child."

A few moments passed. Apperson scratched his head. "Perhaps it is wise to consider all options."

"Now you're making sense," Perry said.

"But where?" Apperson asked Jane.

All eyes turned to her, placing a thousand heavy stones upon her shoulders. "Well . . ." She paused, pondering the question. "Let's find out where we are." She rose and went to the wagon and drew a rolled map from the boot. Returning to the light of the fire, she unfurled it on the ground. All the party crowded around her. The etchings outlined rivers and landmarks of the area. "By my estimate, I would place us here," she said, pointing to a spot east of the Pecos River.

Burroughs squatted next to her. "I'd say you're right, missy. Not far to the south is a trading post." He drew his finger down the map to the west of the river. "It hasn't been there long, but there's people there, a store too. It's run by a cuss named Bean. Calls himself a judge, 'cause there ain't nothing there to say otherwise."

"How far do you guess it might be?" asked Cole.

The ranger took a deep breath. "Thirty miles, maybe less."

"Very well, then," Apperson announced as if a new revelation. "It is there we shall steer for."

"Then where?" Perry's question broke the agreeable mood. "After we go to this post, how long will we continue this charade? What about the next time? Are we to wander in these hills until we run dry of water again?"

"You're free to leave at anytime, Major," Apperson said causally.

"I believe I can answer Major Perry's question, Lord Apperson." Jane pointed to the area west of the Pecos River. "According to the letter, there is a large rock, with instructions as to the chamber's location."

Cole couldn't restrain a chuckle. "Yes, ma'am. There's a few thousand of them. When daylight comes, take a good look. You're surrounded by rocks."

"Not rocks, Mr. Cole. A single rock. '*Piedra aislado*; an isolated stone' is what the letter refers to. So you see, we must find not thousands but only one."

"What nonsense," Perry chided. "You propose to go looking for a single rock?"

Jane held her tongue, although anxious to debate the major. However, the vision required faith to see it, and she realized that those without the virtue would be blind.

"I think I know what you're looking for," Burroughs muttered, and all eyes and interest shot at him, including Jane's. The ranger captain noticed the attention and looked to her and nodded. "Right around here," he said, placing his finger in the center of the area she had circled. "There's an old, dried-up riverbed. Been there longer than I can remember. It's probably a mile wide, and smack dab in the middle is a boulder bigger than a cabin."

"How extraordinary," Apperson said happily. "What a stroke of luck having you in our midst. You must guide us there, Captain Burroughs."

"No," Burroughs said, shaking his head. "I got three men to bury. I aim to do just that as soon as I can find a horse and a wagon to get them laid to rest proper."

"I'll take you to that trading post tomorrow," said Cole.

"And leave us to the tirades of Major Perry?" Apperson scoffed. "No, I most prefer that you take him there, Major. You'll get your wish to divorce yourself from this 'nonsense,' as you call it."

Perry nodded. "I'll be glad to assist."

"No," Mouton said. "It is I who must go. I will take the law officer. It will leave you two trained men with knowledge of the land to take you to the post, Lord Apperson."

The Englishman looked to Burroughs. "I trust there are no objections." Burroughs shook his head and Apperson clapped his hands. "Lovely. Then we should all get a good night's rest." He bid good evening to all those around the fire and went to his tent, followed by his manservant.

Jane stepped closer to Perry. "I guess we'll enjoy your company for a few more days, Major?"

"I meant no disrespect, Doctor." Perry looked at the nearby Cole. "My objective all along has been the safe conclusion of this matter, so I can pursue a more important issue."

Jane sensed some tension between the two men, but her tired eyes convinced her not to involve herself. "Well, if you gentlemen will excuse me, we have a long day ahead, and I agree with Lord Apperson that a night's rest is due. Good night." Both men tipped their hats to her as she went to her tent, putting her arm around Adela, guiding the young girl and child toward a night's sleep.

"I got to get some rest myself," Cole said as he turned to the palomino to retrieve his bedroll, but was stopped by Perry's grip of his arm.

"What happened out there?"

"Like was said, I found the ranger and we snuck up on some Mexicans around a fire."

"Sounds like a sentry is in order," Perry said with a nod.

"Not a bad idea. Wake me in a couple of hours and I'll spell you." Cole turned but was interrupted again.

"Before you go," Perry said, putting his hand in his blouse. "I wasn't going to give you this. But I thought if you had the courage to give me back my revolver, I should have the same to give you this." He drew a envelope with the top torn open. "At the time, I thought it my duty to open it. Now, in light of what's happened and as an officer, I regret the decision. I hope what's in it doesn't alter our agreement, but perhaps urge you to finish this treasure hunt and come back with me as soon as you can. It came not long after you left Nobility in New Mexico. When I learned of it, I commandeered it as evidence."

Cole took the envelope, surprised by Perry's offering both in hand and in mind. To Cole, the written words on the paper inside were a blur of black and white. He would need another act of someone's goodwill to tell him what information it held.

Chapter Eight

With the sun in the eastern sky, Cole looked back at the wagon ruts lined in the dust to the end of the horizon. Having filled the water barrels and all canteens, the party had traveled nearly three miles, and Cole planned to have them at the trading post by the next day's nightfall.

Mouton, with Burroughs riding double, came along side of him. "Don't you two make a bright pair."

Burroughs frowned at the remark. "I would take that burro back there if need be to get those men buried."

A bit sorry for making light of Burroughs's situation, Cole tried to change the subject. "Well, since you two are heading out, just where is this post we're trying to make?"

"Head south and you should start to see the Pecos River. You'll need to follow it till just before it joins up with the Rio Grande. At some point, you'll have to cross it. At that stretch it's mighty wide. With them storms that come through, it's likely plumb full, but there are some shallows you'll find if you look for them hard enough. They'll be rushing fast if my guess is right, but you'll get across them. I have faith in you, Mr. Cole."

"Thanks for the confidence. I'm sure I'll be needing it."

"Just the same, once you get across, head due west, and you'll see train tracks. The Galveston, Harrisburg and San Antonio railroad was building through last I knew. May be there by now. Once you're there, you'll see some tents near the tracks, just ahead of Dead Man's Canyon."

"Where?"

"You heard me. It ain't as bad as all that. Watch your step once you're in the place. Bean runs it from a saloon. He likes to act high and mighty. But he keeps the rascals out."

"I'll remember that. What are you two going to do once you get those men in the ground?"

"I ain't going to leave them there. The damn injuns will just dig them up. We'll bring them in by wikum and meet you there. I'll get them on a train to San'tone." Burroughs looked ahead while Mouton kept his eyes on Cole. "Hell, once this is over, I'll buy you a drink."

"I'll hold you to it," said Cole. Burroughs patted Mouton's shoulder.

Cole watched the two ride to the west. After a moment, he headed back to the wagon. Burroughs's warning weighed heavily in his plans for the journey. Rushing water could prove more deadly to cross than a mountain range in the middle of winter. Once in the middle, there was no sitting still to weather the fury. Recollections of cattle drives ten years ago became clear, where several steers and a drover of two were swept away never to be seen again. It was a tooth-and-nail fight with seldom a chance to turn around.

As he neared the wagon, Major Perry rode parallel to the team and the woman doctor again walked beside the wheels. "The ranger says we'll be crossing the Pecos before long. He thinks it may be high up the bank. I'm riding ahead to find a place to cross."

"I'll go with you," said Perry.

"No, I think it best if you stay here. One of us should keep an eye out for trouble. If either those Comanches or Mexicans come up on you, fire a shot and I'll be back in a hurry."

Perry turned his head with a bit of disgust. He couldn't argue the logic.

"How long do you expect to be?" asked Apperson.

"Not long. Couple of hours at most. I just want to get a look at what's ahead over them rocks."

"I'd like to go, Mr. Cole," Jane said. "I would welcome the chance to get a different view."

Cole shook his head. "That ain't a smart idea, either."

"Oh, I'm sure you wouldn't be burdened with me."

"It ain't all a matter of that. It's hard to know what's over that rise. If I was to run into trouble, I can't say how safe you'd be."

"But you just said the same risk applies here with Major Perry. It seems to me no matter where we might be, until we reach the trading post, none of us is free from threat. So what does it matter if I'm with you?"

A long breath let Cole consider the idea. Trapped as Perry had been, he found himself at a loss to argue her logic. "All right, but just for a short while."

His decision brightened her face. She went to the palomino. Cole removed his right foot from the stirrup so she could climb up. She offered her hand and he pulled her onto the horse's rump. Her long skirt made her sit to the side. The horse took a step to adjust to the weight. The jarring move surprised her and she clumsily grabbed Cole's chest. Once the horse stood firm, Jane seemed reluctant to change her awkward grip. Cole casually moved her hands around his waist.

"You sure you want to do this?" he asked.

"Oh, yes. No complaints here." Her voice was as true to her answer as a thief's claim of innocence.

Cole shook off the incident, hoping it was not an omen for the afternoon. "Rest the horses in another hour," he said to Perry, riding past. He nudged the palomino and steered south.

The afternoon sun glared off the limestone rocks and dust. Jane wiped away the sweat dripping from her brow and nose with her fingers. "May I have some water?" she asked. Cole took the canteen from the horn and handed it back to her. The warm water did little to relieve the heat, but the liquid washed away the parching dust from her throat. She took another gulp and handed the canteen back to him. "How much further?"

He reined in and took a drink himself. "Hard to say, I never been here. Could be around the next rise."

"We've been gone from the others for some time. It seems like hours."

"Well, about half a one is closer to it. The heat has a way of making time slow down." He swiped his sleeve across his chin and neck. "Better give the horse some of this." A moment passed before she realized he meant to give the palomino some water, and she needed to dismount. She attempted to slide gently off the rump, but crashed knees first onto the sand.

"You okay?" His concern came with a small smile; however, the embarrassment just made her nod. He swung his right leg off the palomino and cupped water under its nose. "Ain't what you thought, huh?"

"I beg your pardon?"

"This out here. Ain't the Sunday picnic you thought it would be."

"On the contrary," she said, feeling slighted. "I was aware of the conditions. I had read quite extensively about the region." The single shake of his head proved she wasn't convincing. A confession was in order. "Truthfully," she said, rubbing the dirt from her hands, "I admit it seems more barren than what I had read about Texas."

He capped the canteen and patted the horse. "That's because there's so much of it. Straight north, it flattens out into grassland prairie that stretches clear through to Kansas. A little east of here, the hills are not as steep and they're covered with grass and trees. Over on the Louisiana side it turns to swamp and north of that there's trees bunched in a thicket right into the Ozarks." He threw the stirrup onto the saddle and pulled the slack from the cinch. "If you follow the Rio Grande far enough," he paused and his voice took a somber tone, "you'll run into the sea."

"From your attitude before, I didn't think you cared much for the state."

"Oh, I never said it didn't have its pretty parts." It seemed as if he had more to say, but he stopped and scanned the area. "We better get a move on. I told Perry we'd be back soon, and we haven't even found the river yet."

Serge Mouton reined in the buckskin, staring into the brilliant desolation of stone and sand dotted with small trees and brush. "How much further, do you think?" His question to Chet Burroughs wasn't without knowledge of the answer. He opened his canteen while the ranger considered the reply.

"Don't rightly know. Could be close, but it's

hard to recall the spot. It was getting near sundown when we were attacked. The night plays tricks with a man of my age."

Mouton passed him the canteen. "Maybe it would be good to allow the horse some rest, no?"

"That's a plumb good idea, Frenchy." Burroughs slipped off the horse.

"I am not French," Mouton said quickly in defense of national pride. "I am Belgian."

"No offense intended, friend," said Burroughs. He took a swig of water. "I ain't rightly smart about the difference."

The admission was genuine. Although he was eager to explain the distinction, educating Burroughs wasn't why Mouton had volunteered to come with the Texan. He flashed his wide smile. "It is not a problem, my friend. I myself have trouble with what is Texas and what is Mexico. They were one at one time, yes?"

Burroughs nodded. "That was a long time ago. But it didn't take much for those that settled here to see that they needed to be independent. The Mexicans never had much to do with Texas. They only wanted folks to settle here to keep the Comanche from raiding stock and supplies. Once something was made of the land, that's when Sam Houston and others decided they'd be better off without Mexicans running things. I was just a boy when the fight started, and it's been forty-five years since we sent Santa Anna back with his tail between his legs."

"Ah, I see," said Mouton, nodding. "And Mexico never tried to get Texas again?"

"Oh," Burroughs said before he swallowed another gulp, "they tried, about ten years later. Had themselves a war with America, but it wasn't much of a war. They lost most of what they held north and west of here. Hell, all the land to California belonged to Mexico before the war. They had to sell it just to stop the fighting before they lost everything else."

The lesson in Texas history was interesting, but it wasn't a new one. Mouton had become very familiar with the region's political past. However, its future intrigued him more. "And do you think Texas will belong to Mexico again?"

The idea produced a single chuckle from the Texan. "Not if I ever have anything to do with it." He handed the canteen to Mouton. "Hey, that's a right smart looking rifle you have there. Mind if I look at it?"

"No, please go ahead." Mouton dismounted the buckskin, as Burroughs drew the weapon from the scabbard. "It is the finest of its kind, do you think?"

Burroughs nodded as he examined it closer. "It is a mighty nice piece. Where'd you get it?"

"It is of my own design."

"That a fact? How come it is you make guns?"

The question brought a glare from Mouton. It was not the time to tell everything. "It is a business of my family. We are in service to most of the countries in Europe." The answer did not appear to satisfy the ranger's curiosity. More questions could ask Mouton to reveal more than he wished. The matter of the journey was an easy subject on which to focus. "When do think we will reach the bodies of your men?" he said casually, regaining the rifle.

A moment passed before the answer came. "That might be hard to know from here." Burroughs looked in all directions, then stared at a small rocky plateau and pointed. "Let me have a look-see from the top of them rocks. I'll get a better view from there."

The ranger walked to the perch, removing his hat to wipe sweat from his brow. Mouton squinted into the sun and concentrated on the Texan's back while methodically removing a magazine from the pouch and loading it into the rifle. His hands inched into position, fingers wrapping around the wooden handle on the barrel. Burroughs stepped from one rock up to another as Mouton pulled the loading bolt back to propel the first bullet into the chamber. The older man shaded his eyes from the glare to search for the location of his lost brethren. Mouton raised the rifle, butting the stock against his right shoulder. While squeezing the trigger, he muttered, "Farewell, my friend."

Major Perry's head snapped around in the direction of a distant pop echoing from over the high rocks. "Did you hear that?"

Apperson paused in sipping his tea. "Hear what, Major?"

"That sounded like a shot." Although he scanned the surroundings, the only sights were the old Englishman in his chair, the red faced Jeffers busily feeding a small fire and the girl Adela holding a bucket from which the stock could drink.

"I didn't hear anything." Apperson shrugged, as did his butler. "Perhaps you're hearing things, Major Perry. Happens to the best of us. It's the desert playing tricks with you."

"I know I heard something, your *lordship*," Perry sniped. "I'm quite used to the sounds of the wilderness, and that wasn't one of them."

"Very well, then. Perhaps you should investigate. It could be one of our friends trying to signal us, needing our help to get away from trouble of some sort."

"That would be foolish," Perry said, shaking his head. "We're surrounded by unfriendly forces. Our best defense is to stay together, not separate."

"You sound as if we're at war."

"We are at war." Perry peered into Apperson's eyes. He couldn't hold his opinion any longer. "You fail to recognize that, sir. We're at least a hundred miles from the nearest military post. We've been told of not only hostile renegades, but of Mexican rebels raiding near here. Our only defense is this pistol and an antique shotgun. Hardly enough to hold off a small band, much less a large one. We're low on food, ammunition, our water is vulnerable, we're hindered by a woman and child. We are primed for attack. And I must admit I am disgusted by your cavalier manner. It's as if you think this is all a game, a charade, able to be dismissed at any time. I am a soldier, sir. Trained to anticipate trouble. You, on the other hand, seem to invite it."

Apperson applauded. "Well said, man. Well said. You should enter politics. A real knack for assessing the current state of affairs, you have. Well, I think lunch may be ready."

A deep breath restrained Perry's anger. Past commanders had the same ambivalence toward his field reports. Army code of conduct prevented him from airing his objections, but he'd been warned that his distressed demeanor bordered on insubordination. Although promotion to major was an extreme achievement following the Civil War, friends in the officer corps remarked his attitude cost him the rank of colonel.

Another long sigh testified to the realization that further words of caution would be futile. He knelt next to the fire and took a cup of water from Jeffers.

Apperson drew a small flask from his pocket and dashed his tea with the contents. A suggestive rise in the Englishman's eyebrows offered the courtesy of spicing Perry's cup. Officers were forbidden from any liquor on duty, however, the present circumstance—disobeying orders to report to his post—brought the silent admission he was no longer an officer or soldier. He nodded and Apperson gleefully shared the spirits.

The trenchant taste awoke senses long dormant. He took a longer sip. He finished the cup with a gulp, and the thought that alcohol was best taken with food made him reach for a piece of the dried beef and prop his hat back.

The brilliant light had softened, and notice of Apperson's quizzical attention on something behind him halted his bite.

"What on earth is that?" muttered Apperson.

Perry faced about, frozen by the cool breeze and oncoming onslaught. "Mr. Jeffers, secure the camp and tie everything down. Turn the wagon broadside and tether the team to it. We have only a minute at best!"

The long rumbled ride gnashing her bones forced Jane to rethink her decision to see the land. Much of her view was limited to Cole's back, and the heat produced a pungent odor. At first, she presumed it came from the horse or maybe him. Now, it was even possible she had absorbed the stench.

"Shouldn't we turn back?"

"Wouldn't do us much good to make this trip twice."

Although it was a prudent response, she had hoped for a more sympathetic one. She wiped sweat from her cheeks again. She had sweated more that day than the entire time she was in Texas. "I regret to ask again—"

"The river should be close, according to what the ranger said. Do you need a rest?"

"Yes, please." Cole reined in the horse, this time careful to hold her arm and ease her to the ground. He came off the horse and handed her the canteen.

The tepid water never tasted so sweet. After

the initial gulp, she raised the canteen for another long gulp, but Cole took it from her.

"Too much too quick on a hot stomach and it'll come gushing back up." He allowed the palomino some water. She stood, disturbed at his choice of priorities, but quickly realized the horse's well-being superseded her own at the moment. Cole poured more into his cupped palm, took his own small slurp and handed the canteen back to her.

Careful to heed his advice, she wet her pursed lips and took small sips. "You're very good with animals, aren't you?"

"Some more than others." He patted the palomino's flanks. "If you take care of them, they'll take care of you." His eyes showed a reflection of kindness she hadn't expected from a man with such a hardened face.

"You know, when I was a little girl, I wanted to be a veterinary doctor. Then my father reminded me that all I was likely to see were the sick and dying. Once I thought of the prospect of a cute kitten suffering, I decided that wasn't for me."

"Sounds like a smart choice," he said to the ground. "It ain't never easy to put one down that's been with you a while." After a moment, he raised his head. "It's about time we gave him a rest. We'll walk some ways. You like walking, don't you?" His question came with a smirk, which she returned.

She followed him as they headed toward a cragged escarpment rising from the desert floor.

"I was wondering, if you don't mind me asking," she said, pausing to keep her balance upon the rocky soil. A second thought cautioned her not to ask, but she needed to know. "Have you ever 'put down,' as you call it, another man?"

"When forced to," he answered casually without turning around. It was as if she asked him his name.

"How many?"

He stopped and faced her. She stopped as well, sure she had broached a subject she was likely to regret when he narrowed his eyes.

"Why do you want to know?"

Instantly, she felt alone, surrounded by acres of desolation. Why had she asked such a question? Her heartbeat quickened. She couldn't keep from glancing at the gun strapped to his hip. After a few calm seconds, when his hand made no move to draw the weapon, she resumed breathing and cracked an inquisitive grin. "Curiosity?"

He shook his head slightly. "It ain't something I take pride in. Not like I keep count. Is that what you think of me? One of them that cuts notches in pistol grips?"

"No. Of course not."

He twisted about and resumed his purposeful stride. She had to increase her step just to stay the same distance behind.

"Mr. Cole. Clay." She stopped again, realizing she couldn't keep up. He kept walking. "I didn't mean it as an offense. I was just wondering.

I've heard stories of men in the West, and I thought it might be something you wanted to tell me."

He continued up the small slope, which crested at the base of the escarpment. Once at the top, he stopped and looked into the distance. Her lonesome feeling returned, only now, instead of being shot, she was afraid he would abandon her in this wasteland without a clue as to how to find the way back to the wagon. Finally, he turned to her. She stared at his figure atop the hill.

"Are you coming?" he called. She raised her hem so as to scurry the distance before he could have a change of heart. With perspiration dripping into her eyes and the dry air searing her breath, she trudged up the incline to stand next to him.

"Thirsty?" The trite question didn't deter her answering.

"Terribly."

He didn't reach for the canteen still draped to the saddle, but instead pointed down the other end of the slope. She looked to see a beautiful winding river. The water's flow was strong, cascading over large rocks, the waves shimmering in the sunlight.

She put her hand to her blouse to settle her pounding heart and guffawed at the delightful sight. "You did it! You found the river."

"Yeah, and none to soon. Even looks like we came to a place to cross by the looks of them rocks. Can't be too deep." He led the palomino down the grade. She carefully descended behind to arrive at the bank. Never had simple water seemed such a blessing.

She flung her hat to her side and scooped a drink, then another, and another, until instinct had her dip both hands full and splash her face and neck. Closing her eyes, she allowed the chill to caress her scorched cheeks. The soothing relief soon dripped under her collar to cool her flesh beneath her underclothes. Another splash down her back provided even more refreshment. Religion had never been a strong belief, but at the moment she couldn't think of a finer deliverance.

She opened her eyes to see Cole knee-deep in the stream, staring at her. She could feel the breeze press against her wet skin. He grunted and turned his back and she peeked at her saturated blouse outlining her feminine form. Immediately crossing her arms, she rose and faced about, her cheeks flush.

"It'll be some time before the horse is rested enough to go back."

She appreciated his announcement. It would give her clothes time to dry, but likely not enough to regain her dignity. She sank her face in her palm. Crying would only worsen the matter, so she walked along the bank to escape his view. Even when several yards away, she could sense his presence, but she dared not stray beyond the near bend. She sat on a flat rock that protruded above the scrub brush nurtured by the river.

As soon as she regained a normal pulse, a rustle in the bushes sent it throbbing. At first she froze still until another thrashing of branches made her squeal and charge off the rock.

The noise followed her. She ran off the bank into the water's edge. Cole ran onto the shore. In one fluid motion, he drew the pistol and aimed at arm's length to fire. Sparks and smoke exploded from the muzzle. The shot bellowed off the rock walls. Her ears rang at a continual high pitch.

She glanced at him, and he at her for only a moment. He went to the rock with gun still steadied in front and once there, he let out breath, then a slight giggle. "Well," he said, reaching into the brush and lifting tail first a blood-dripped carcass the size of a small dog. "At least it's dead."

Upon recognizing the animal's bony plated hide she slumped her shoulders. "An *armadillo?*"

"No. It's an armadilla."

"I know what it is." She stopped herself before bothering to argue. "*Dasypus novemcinctus.* A burrowing, insect-eating mammal."

Cole gave her a strange stare, then aimed the same expression at the animal. "I call it dinner."

As she took a step, her foot slipped into a depression. The clear water allowed her to peer below the surface at the shape of an odd cavity more than a yard wide. It wasn't round, but oblong with three distinct protrusions at one end and a single larger one at the other. She knelt and felt its firm edges. It wasn't silt or sand. It was rock.

"Oh, my Lord," she muttered in awe. Cole was soon standing over her as she continued to marvel at the discovery. "Do you know what this is?"

"A hole?"

"Not just a hole. Look at the shape. It's a footprint. Dinosaur tracks. Massive reptiles. Probably a quadruped herbivore. I read about fossils found in Montana by Dr. Cope."

"A what?"

"A four-legged plant eater, like a cow. Only much larger."

"Well, no matter what name you give that varmint, by the size of that track, I don't want to be here when it comes back."

"I wouldn't worry," she said, feeling a grin cross her face. "They're extinct. They all died millions of years ago, it's believed. But that 'arma-dil-lo' is a descendant. These animals had those same plates."

Cole took another long stare at his bounty. "Them plates aren't the only thing this one has in common with them. This one is 'extinct' too." His grin made Jane smile. He turned for shore.

"Don't you want to get a closer look?"

"Well, I've already seen more than I should."

His peculiar remark puzzled her. "I don't understand."

"You ain't dry," he said with his back to her.

She instantly looked to her blouse, which still clearly showed through to her camisole. Again feeling a fool, she turned away and peeked over her shoulder at him. This humiliation didn't hurt her dignity as much as injure her pride. She as much as invited him to gaze at her body, perhaps lending the impression she was a loose woman. On some level, it may have been her intent. She recalled the words of her father, discouraging her ambition, chiding that if her first love was to her career, no man would want to be second and she would likely end up a spinster.

She watched Cole walk to the horse. There was something about this man she couldn't put into words. He didn't seem to fit the image of a scurrilous Westerner she'd heard about, who could have exploited her predicament. But even without the manner of a formal gentleman, this man showed a more important courtesy not often shown women, even in the East—respect. Not just today, nor this moment, but since they had met. To say the least, he was different. He was unique.

"We best be getting back," he said. "We spent more time trying to find this spot than I figured."

She silently agreed and rose from the water with arms still firmly crossed. Although they were quite damp, the heat would dry her clothes by the time they reached camp, and during the ride, his back would be to her.

By the time she stood next to him, he had tied the kill to the pommel. After removing the pistol, he discarded the spent cartridge and replaced it with a fresh one.

"Expecting trouble?" she asked.

"Never know when you'll need another shot."

He stepped into the stirrup, steering his eyes from her. He hesitated, then removed his foot and turned to her with exasperation.

"Get back to the rocks," he ordered.

"Why? What's wrong?"

"You see that?" he said, pointing to the west. A brown haze shrouded the sun. "Sandstorm. The wind whips it so hard, it'll skin you alive." He slipped the bandanna over his nose.

She ran down the shore with him right behind her steps. She sensed the sunlight fading. He passed her, one hand leading the horse by the reins, the other snatching her arm. His firm grasp almost lifted her off her feet. The air became coarse and heavy. A gust instantly flattened the river's waves. A tremendous force impelled her from behind, almost shoving her down if not for his steady support. They continued up the bank toward the base of the escarpment, battling the increasing gale for their balance.

Once they reached the towering rock, sand pelted her arms, legs, and face. "Cover your eyes," he yelled over the howling wind and the palomino's whinnies. She did so just as they began to burn and her hands felt as if the skin were being grated off them. He led her to the far side to shield them from the torrent of dust.

As the assault lessened, she opened her eyes and tried to brush the sand from her blurry sight. "What'll we do?"

He pushed her into a cavity in the rock barely large enough for both of them and the horse. As her focus improved, she noticed the plain before them. Small bushes bent to the ground were becoming obscured by curtains of sand. The sunshine was all but gone, forming an eerie twilight.

Chapter Nine

The blistering wind sank Mouton to his knees. Squinted eyes allowed barely enough light to see but were quickly closed so as not to be blinded by the sand. Only once had he been through something like this. He had to remind himself that this was Texas, not the Sahara.

With the reins torn from his grasp by the fleeing buckskin, he had no hope of escaping the storm. He chose to hide behind an dune emerging from the windswept plain. Cradling his rifle close to his chest, he hoped to lessen the contamination in the firing lock. The coat's lapel drawn over his nose gave him few filtered breaths.

The plan to rejoin the others now seemed unreasonable. The storm must have captured them as well, and it was doubtful they would search for him. Military training forced him on elbows and knees along the edge of the dune to find some break from the tempest. To survive he would have to find shelter, then water.

The sand collapsed beneath him. The dune to his back quickly fell away into a slope, sliding him down an embankment into a crevice. It served as a trench that shielded him from the wind. Believing it to be a divine intervention, he pulled back the lapel to inhale large gasps of clear air. The salvation passed quickly upon the blurred view of leather-wrapped feet inches away. As he blinked away the sand, he saw legs in a firm stance, then a waist, hands holding a rifle, a shirt of red hue and long black hair surrounding a dark face.

Cole slowly rotated the armadillo carcass suspended by a rock-and-stick spit over the open fire. Jane had endured the putrid odor during the skinning of the animal. She was moments away from fainting when he stoked the entrails into the burgeoning fire. However, once the tissue fueled the coals to ignite into flame, the smell quickly dissipated with help from the breeze swirling about the cavity.

"It's still raging," she said, peering outside.

"Ain't nothing going to stop it until it blows through," he replied without looking at her.

"I wonder how the others are."

He propped back his hat and spoke with a slight nod. "Been thinking about that myself. Unless they found cover, they likely got the worst of it." He let out a deep breath. "But

Perry's been through worse than this. I would think he used the wagon as a windbreak. I'm sure he got them through it."

She didn't believe his evaluation entirely. Gauging the fierce winds whipping just a few feet from her, she knew better than to expect the harsh conditions had put only minor distress on Adela and her infant, the aging Jeffers and even Lord Apperson. However, she tried to put it from her mind. There was little she could do for them except hope for the best. In a way, Cole's reassurance had done what he had intended it to do.

"Yes, I'm sure you're right. Major Perry's experience would be quite invaluable. I'm sure he's been involved in considerable trials as a soldier."

Cole continued to stare at the fire. "That he has," he muttered. "Lord knows, he's like a snake. Once he takes to swallowing something, he can't let go." He took the canteen and swigged a gulp. "I can swear to that."

By his almost pained expression, it seemed the remark wasn't meant as flattery. He offered the canteen and she took it. "If I may ask, just what is the trouble between you two? I confess, I'm confused by you both. At one point, the two of you are enemies. He claimed he was your prisoner. At the next morning, you appeared having settled your differences."

"It is strange, ain't it?" he answered, then removed his hat to scratch his head. "I guess when you've known a man as long as I've known him, you get so used to each other. It's kind of like a partnership." He paused, dipping his eyes to the ground. "But we ain't on the same side of the stakes and it ain't friendly."

"How do you mean that?" she asked, then took a sip.

He rotated the spit again, taking time before answering. "You might say, we both got something we need to get settled."

"With what he said? About charges against you for treason?"

He nodded. Drippings from the roast spattered bits of flame and sparks. Wisps of smoke and waning sizzles seemed to come from him as much as it did the fire. "That's the part about having different stakes." He drew the knife and sliced a small portion from the roast. He ripped it in two and offered her the other.

She accepted it with her fingertips, reluctant at first to sample the meat for fear of the unknown, but hunger won over and she nibbled enough to taste. Never having eaten more exotic meats than poultry or beef, she found the flavor tolerable, resembling pork or chicken. The more she nibbled, the more she wanted. "This is quite good."

"Most things are if you give them a try."

His reasoning seemed profound. It could apply to more than just wild game. When resheathing the knife, a rumble came from his pocket. Seeming a bit surprised by the noise, he drew a small envelope.

"A letter?" she asked.

"Yeah," he answered with a less enthusiastic expression.

"From a relative, perhaps?"

"I, uh, ain't read it."

"Really? Whenever I receive a letter, I can't wait to rip it open and devour every word."

He shook his head. "I never got in the habit."

"Why is that?" She sensed the answer almost as soon as she asked the question. His darting eyes convinced her to ask another. "You can't read, can you?" A few quiet moments passed before he looked her in the eye the same way as when asked about his past with a gun.

"No, ma'am. I can't."

The admission came with some visible anguish. She thought it courageous. Although a simple task, it appeared to be one of very few skills this man of the frontier didn't possess and he appeared to take no pride in his lack of it. A polite proposal would be a rare favor she could render.

"I'd be glad to read it for you."

Tapping the envelope in his palm, he pondered the suggestion. Finally, he extended it around the flame to her. "I'd guess I'd be obliged to you."

The top had been split open. The script appeared to come from a delicate pen stroke. Curiosity had her flip the single page over. The signature confirmed her suspicion. "Do you know someone named Claire Rhodes?"

His jaw slipped open. He blinked twice then nodded.

Although accustomed to reading silently, Jane realized it would be rude. It wasn't her letter, so she read aloud.

November 8, 1879

Dearest Clay, I cannot express how I welcomed the news when Father told me you had contacted him. It is my sincerest hope that you are safe and at peace. My better sense tells me that might not be the case. My return journey was long and tiresome as had been the trip to Colorado. However, along the way I made two fortunate discoveries. The first is one only a woman would know. A final blessing from my marriage from John. I hope to share more news within the next year.

The second is a matter concerning you. I met a man on the train in Ohio proclaiming his desire to be our next president. In my conversation with him, I recounted what you had told me about the events surrounding you and the death of Colonel Custer. He said he would be willing to review the matter thoroughly and thought the issue of a pardon might be possible, if elected, of course. Even though I cannot vote, I am campaigning for Mr. J. A. Garfield in hopes of him fulfilling that promise.

I'll do what can be done. I owe you my life, and the life of another I cannot mention as yet. May God keep you safe.

Forever your close friend,
Claire Rhodes

Jane carefully folded the note and replaced it in the envelope. "She seems quite devoted to you," she said, handing him the letter. "Who is she? What did she mean about you and Colonel Custer?"

"This ain't a story I brag about telling." He tucked the letter into his pocket.

It was apparent the memory pained him. Nonetheless, if she could get him to talk, it might ease some of the anguish. "What if I promised not to brag about hearing it?"

The question brought a smirk to his face. "Hell, more people know now than I ever cared to know it."

He drew the knife again and sliced a larger piece of the roast and gave it to her, then cut himself one of equal size. The pause seemed to allow him to collect his thoughts.

"I was a scout with the Seventh Cavalry under the command of Lieutenant Colonel George A. Custer. I was at the Little Big Horn. When Custer came down that hill, I was on the wrong side of the river."

"I don't understand. What do you mean the wrong side?"

He chewed on the meat and began to slice another when his eyes met hers. "On one side there was the Seventh. And on the other there was the Sioux."

She found it hard to believe and hard to breathe. The lonely surroundings again encompassed her. Had she stumbled across a subject she would regret? Had she sparked a fire she couldn't put out? "So? It is true?"

His head dipped down, then looking at her with pursed lips, he shook his head.

She let out a long-held breath. "Well, then I'm still confused. What did she mean in this letter? Who is this woman?"

"She was a lady from the East I helped out in Colorado."

"Well, it seems as if you did more than just help her out," said Jane after accepting another slice of the meat.

"She had gone out there to meet up with her husband. I got a wire from a man, said it was her father, a fellow named Thorsberg from Baltimore—"

"Jacob Thorsberg! The shipping magnate?"

"Yeah," he answered as if reminded of something. "She said he had something to do with ships."

"He's one of the richest men in the country." She was amazed at the mere mention. "He controls most of the shipping and ship building on the entire Eastern waterfront. Yes, I would agree. He has quite a lot to do with ships. And this Claire is his daughter?"

"Yup. Like I was saying, he sent me a letter offering a thousand dollars if I would take her up to her husband's mine in the old mining hills in southwest Colorado. But it turned out her husband partnered up with a land cheat. He was the one told her to come out there so he could take her money. She brought all she had. She didn't know no better."

"And you saved her," Jane said, hoping that too was true.

He nodded with a bit of modesty. "I helped her out. Rid the living of a few no-goods while I was at it. But her husband got killed by the partner. She said later that he didn't seem like her husband no more. Life in them hills will change a fellow."

"So that is why she is so indebted to you."

"I guess." He resheathed the knife. "It didn't start out that way, but we got to know each other pretty good."

While considering the possibilities of his answer, another thought occurred to her. "It could be that she has done what she set out to do."

"Huh? I don't follow."

"Well, this letter is dated more than a year and half ago. Mr. Garfield is the president." His puzzled expression made her explain. "He was sworn in office in March. I read it in the papers of San Antonio."

"So, what you're saying . . ."

"What I'm saying is it is possible she has campaigned for your pardon. A president can do that, you know."

Slowly his face began to turn. The hardened nature faded into a contemplative relief. A small grin slowly edged across his lips. It was clear the idea of amnesty had never occurred to him. His reaction was infectious and she began to feel the same joy. At that moment, Jane said a silent prayer. It was only human to wish the best for another. If only it had come to pass.

"Will there be anything else, Mrs. Rhodes?"

Claire continued to stare out her window

overlooking the Chesapeake. Her maid's persistence interrupted her thoughts. "Is everything prepared for the ladies' luncheon this afternoon?"

"Yes, ma'am. Cook is preparing halibut in lemon-and-parsley sauce just as you ordered."

"Very well," she said, looking at the servant. "I want everything to go smoothly. We'll be putting the final plans together for the Independence Day gala tomorrow. Has the newspaper arrived?"

"Yes, ma'am. It's on the table in the foyer."

Duties of a society maven had fallen firmly on her shoulders since her mother nominated her to head the Baltimore Women's Society. The post was taxing on her time, but it never crept above her highest priority. "Oh, Penny," she blurted, turning the maid's attention to her. "Is he sleeping?"

"Yes, ma'am," was the smiling answer. "Master Stuart went down for his nap about a half hour ago."

"Thank you, Penny. You may go." The maid left the room and Claire went to her closet. With never enough time in a day to accomplish all her goals, she quickly picked through her wardrobe for the proper gown. Attire showed taste. As she flipped through the garments, she stopped once, touching a favorite dress of blue taffeta. Her heart beat a little quicker as memories filled her head. It was the dress she wore upon her arrival in Platte Falls, Colorado.

Her experiences at the other end of the country were bittersweet. She had risked her life to join her husband, whom she barely recognized either in mind or in body. It was an ill-advised adventure she'd been warned about by others, including her father. She feared his boastful reaction when she returned, only to arrive pleasantly pleased with loving acceptance without a word said.

It made it all the easier to tell the tale of her long trip, watching the majestic landscape pass by train-car windows, the rugged life she witnessed of men with guns as part of their clothes, how she very nearly lost her own life, once by a bullet that her once beloved husband, John, stepped in front of as the single and last act of his love, and another time clutching to life on a rocky cliff the locals called Danger Ridge.

Just as in the adage of clouds with silver linings, she again recalled her parents' overjoyed surprise when she announced she had come home carrying John's child. She too was surprised when the possibility was whispered in her ear by a traveling matron as explanation of the nausea after breakfast. It was then she remembered her last night with John weeks earlier. Preferring to look upon it as a blessing of love, she hadn't told her parents nor would she ever tell her son of John's brutal act of drunkenness that brought about the conception.

The favor was returned when her father told her the man who saved her life had telegrammed for the fee promised him for his service. The true price for his deeds couldn't be paid in money, although her father had wired

EXPERIENCE THE ADVENTURE
AND THE DRAMA OF THE OLD WEST
WITH THE GREATEST WESTERNS
ON THE MARKET TODAY...
FROM LEISURE BOOKS

As a home subsriber to the Leisure Western Book Club, you'll enjoy the most exciting new voices of the Old West, plus classic works by the masters in new paperback editions. Every month Leisure Books brings you the best in Western fiction, from Spur-Award-winning, quality authors. Upcoming book club releases include new-to-paperback novels by such great writers as:

Max Brand   Robert J. Conley   Gary McCarthy   Judy Alter
Frank Roderus   Douglas Savage   G. Clifton Wisler
David Robbins   Douglas Hirt

as well as long out-of-print classics by legendary authors like:

Will Henry   T.V. Olsen   Gordon D. Shirreffs

 Each Leisure Western breaths life into the cowboys, the gunfighters, the homesteaders, the mountain men and the Indians who fought to survive in the vast frontier. Discover for yourself the excitement, the power and the beauty that have been enthralling readers each and every month.

SAVE BETWEEN $3.00 AND $6.00
EACH TIME YOU BUY!

Each month, the Leisure Western Book Club brings you four terrific titles from Leisure Books, America's leading publisher of Western fiction. EACH PACKAGE WILL SAVE YOU BETWEEN $3.00 AND $6.00 FROM THE BOOKSTORE PRICE! And you'll never miss a new title with our convenient home delivery service.

 Here's how it works. Each package will carry a FREE* 10-DAY EXAMINATION privilege. At the end of that time, if you decide to keep your books, simply pay the low invoice price of $13.44, ($14.50 US in Canada) no shipping or handling charges added.* HOME DELIVERY IS ALWAYS FREE*. With this price it's like getting one book free every month.

AND YOUR FIRST FOUR-BOOK SHIPMENT
IS TOTALLY FREE*!
IT'S A BARGAIN YOU CAN'T BEAT!

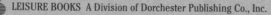 LEISURE BOOKS A Division of Dorchester Publishing Co., Inc.

GET YOUR 4
FREE* BOOKS NOW—
A VALUE BETWEEN
$16 AND $20

Mail the Free* Book Certificate Today!

Tear here and mail your FREE* book card today!

FREE* BOOKS
CERTIFICATE!

YES! I want to subscribe to the Leisure Western Book Club. Please send me my 4 FREE* BOOKS. Then, each month, I'll receive the four newest Leisure Western Selections to preview FREE* for 10 days. If I decide to keep them, I will pay the Special Member's Only discounted price of just $3.36 each, a total of $13.44 ($14.50 US in Canada). This saves me between $3 and $6 off the bookstore price. There are no shipping, handling or other charges.* There is no minimum number of books I must buy and I may cancel the program at any time. In any case, the 4 FREE* BOOKS are mine to keep—at a value of between $17 and $20!

*In Canada, add $5.00 Canadian shipping and handling per order for first shipment. For all subsequent shipments to Canada the cost of membership in the Book Club is $14.50 US, which includes $7.50 shipping and handling per month. All payments must be made in US currency.

Name _____

Address _____

City_____ State_____ Country_____

Zip_____ Telephone_____

If under 18, parent or guardian must sign. Terms, prices and conditions subject to change. Subscription subject to acceptance. Leisure Books reserves the right to reject any order or cancel any subscription.

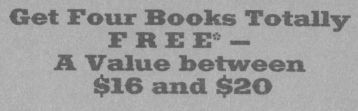

Get Four Books Totally
F R E E* –
A Value between
$16 and $20

Tear here and mail your FREE* book card today!

PLEASE RUSH
MY FOUR FREE*
BOOKS TO ME
RIGHT AWAY!

LeisureWestern Book Club
P.O. Box 6613
Edison, NJ 08818-6613

AFFIX
STAMP
HERE

five thousand dollars upon reading Claire's letter that she was returning to Baltimore. The addition was intended as a bonus for convincing her that life in the West wasn't one meant for her. She knew better. No words played a part in her decision, although it wasn't easy to make.

As a witness to John's killing, she knew she couldn't remain in a land where the law was ruled by men with guns, and whoever held the most guns ruled the law. However, she almost stayed, and likely would have if she had been asked by the man Westerners called the Rainmaker. She knew him as Clay Cole.

Taking the dress into her hands, she held it across her robed body. Her size had changed with motherhood, but with alteration the dress could fit once again. The fashion wasn't quite current, but she didn't have the heart to discard it. Another fond memory sent her to the jewelry box atop the dresser. She opened it. The gold mounted ruby brooch was still there just where she had placed it when she returned from the West. It was a keepsake not only of her family but of her memory of him.

The time in between had changed her circumstances considerably. Not only did she represent her family's social presence, she had also assumed more responsibilities of her father's business since a stroke had left him bedridden the last two months. Vowing never to compromise time spent with her son left little time for any private ambitions. However, she felt compelled to pursue a special one.

On many occasions she had made the short

journey to Washington. Her father's relationships in politics had assisted her to meet many of those who controlled the country. Using that to her advantage had allowed the opportunity to obtain an invitation to the inaugural ball. A few precious moments with the new president gave her enough time to remind him of a previous conversation. Like a gentleman, he said he recalled the discussion. A discussion about a man with a dubious but unwarranted reputation, and the issue of an executive pardon was worth review. She received only another promise to continue the matter at a more convenient time. An appointment was made, and now a quick glance at the calendar reminded her she would be in the capital in one month from the day.

She saw her smile in the mirrored image. The daydream had gotten the best of her and she only had hours before her guests would arrive. Quickly, she put the dress across the bed, shut the jewelry box and hurried back into the closet. In little time, she had put on a dress respectful of the lady of the manor. Another glimpse in the mirror assured her it wasn't too alluring, yet still showed femininity. At least she had shed the black of mourning.

She tiptoed past the nursery, not able to resist a peek of her slumbering pride and joy. Once downstairs, she inspected the foyer and found it in its usual immaculate condition. On her way to do the same with the south parlor, she noticed the newspaper on a table. She picked it up and unfurled the crease so as to view the morning headline.

Shocking news set her heart pounding inside her chest. Her trembling hands shook the paper until she could no longer hold it still and it fell to the floor. Unable to believe the tragic three word banner, she cupped her hands over her mouth. Soon she tasted her own tears. She couldn't imagine it was true.

Chapter Ten

Jane accepted Cole's hand and took her position behind him on the palomino. The morning light revealed the night's carnage. Sand dunes sculpted by the wind's force appeared as petrified sea waves. Sparse signs of green poked over the dust in almost defiant resistance against nature's tyranny.

As the horse stepped down the incline, she was reminded of the few hours of sleep on the ground. She had thought the tent cot was uncomfortable, but compared to the aches she now felt, it would feel like a bed of feathers.

With canteens already filled, Cole steered the mount back to the north to search for the wagon. The storm had cooled the air; however, after more than an hour in the saddle and without her hat, the sun's continual baking of the landscape and of her skin felt little different from the day before. "Where do you think they are?"

"I was looking forward to finding them in the same direction I left them. No promise about that, though."

The distorted air rose from the rocky ground ahead. She looked to the west, where only the peaks of distant mesas edged over the horizon. The river seemed a memory from long ago. Her throat already felt dry. "May I have some water?" He handed her the canteen. After two gulps, she handed it back to him, "I'd never thought water could taste so good."

"Yeah, I know what you mean. There's been a few times I thought I'd never taste it again." He took a quick swig. "We'll keep parallel of the Pecos for about a mile out. Don't want to have to look for it twice."

"That seems wise. This is quite a formidable land without the prospect of water."

He leaned back to talk over his shoulder. "Makes you wonder if that Cortés fellow hid his gold here with that in mind."

"Actually, he didn't. It was the Aztecs who stored their precious belongings here."

"That's right, you said that. You never did tell me why they did him a favor if he treated them so bad."

"No one yet knows why. There are some journals about the relationship between Cortés and the Aztecs, especially that of him and the ruler Montezuma. They seemed to have admired one another."

"I thought you said that he put the chief in chains."

"Yes, however, the presumption is Montezuma didn't protest. In fact, that is how he died. Killed by his own people once he tried to calm them. The mistreatment of the Aztecs wasn't by Cortés hand, but rather by the men he left in charge when he went to meet Narvaez. In fact, most records show that Cortés held a respect for the Aztec people, which was very unusual for the conquistadors of his time. He didn't enslave them as was other tribes' fate. He paid them, if only a token amount. It was only after he was deposed that the true brutality began."

"De-posed? What's that mean?"

"Removed from authority."

"Fired, you mean."

She giggled. "Yes, that is about the same thing in a way."

"They didn't like the job he was doing."

"Yes," she said, again amused. "You have a remarkable way of simplifying matters, Clay." She thought a moment. "Yes, his rivals convinced the king that he couldn't be trusted completely. After all, he did usurp, ah, go over the head of his once friend Velázquez to try and establish himself as governor of what became Mexico. Those type of acts aren't looked upon kindly by those in power."

"Not following orders? I know how that is. What about that woman you keep mentioning?"

"Marina? Not much is known of her after Cortés left for Spain."

He arched around at her. "That a fact?"

"Oh, yes. The Spanish never approved of his relationship with her. Especially after what happened with his wife."

"What might that be?" he said, facing forward.

"She arrived in Mexico some time after Cortés. A member of a wealthy family, she didn't take well to the harsh conditions, nor did she care for Cortés's fathering another woman's children. She was quite vocal about it. Everyone knew of her complaints. She would be what's known as a shrew."

"So she took her man back home, huh?"

"No," Jane answered in a matter of fact tone. "She was found dead on her bed soon after she arrived."

Cole arched about in the saddle with a surprised expression on his face. "Is that a fact? She was killed?"

"No one knows exactly. It is said that Cortés didn't mourn her loss."

Cole cocked his head to the side as he straightened. "Sounds like he cared more for that Marina woman than people knew. I know some men like that. They take up Indian ways, mix with their people, taking squaws as wives, having young'uns with them. They get to be more Indian than their own kind."

The comment caught Jane's attention and sparked her curiosity. "Have you ever taken a wife?"

There was an awkward silence before he answered. "Nope."

Cole appeared ill at ease. Her question must

have seemed like prying, something she was as uncomfortable with as her jarring ride on the horse's rump. On second thought, the animal's end was an appropriate reference.

"There was one once, but we never married," he said, keeping his eyes forward.

Since he responded, she thought to inquire more. "Was she Indian?"

"No." His tone showed the topic pained him. "But she was a woman most proper folk didn't take to just the same. She earned her living in a saloon. I guess it ain't polite to tell you all that she did there. Anyway, she gave it up once we took a shine to each other. Probably ain't polite telling just how that happened neither."

His amusement brought a bit of cheer to the conversation, but it disappeared quickly. He spoke in an ominous cadence.

"But it was Wyoming in winter. It's miserable cold up there. To stay alive you have to keep a fire going most all the time. One day when I weren't there, some kindling was on the floor. And somehow it got too close to the flame . . ."

The result became obvious to her. "I'm so sorry. Forgive me for making you recall such a horrible memory."

"No harm done. Time has a way of taking some of the sting out of it. Her name was Pauline, but I called her Polly."

Jane turned her head away at the thought of the awful incident, regretting she ever broached the subject. She tried to put it from her mind, until he turned the tables.

"What about you, Jane Reeves. You ever take up with a man?"

Surprised by his forward question, she felt a reply deserved, no matter how self-conscious it made her. After all, she wasn't a hypocrite. "I'm afraid not. There never seemed enough time with my studies."

"You must have been around a lot of blind men, not to snatch up a young woman as yourself."

"Well, I appreciate the flattery. But there aren't any men at Vassar, much less blind ones. It's a school only for women."

"That sounds like a waste."

The comment alarmed her. A familiar refrain often repeated by men she did know. "You don't believe in a woman's ability to gain an education?"

"No, ma'am. It ain't that at all. I come to learn that most women can soak up more than most men. I was talking about cooping them all up in one place by themselves."

"Not by our own choice, I assure you. That is a policy set by most men's colleges. They didn't want women intruding in their domain."

"Well," he said as he stood in the stirrups as if to peer in the distance, "like I said, some of the things we do ain't too bright." The delight of his comment didn't last long. He sat back on the saddle. "You best hold on tight. We need to move fast."

His hand firmly wrapped hers around him to hold her steady as he spurred the palomino to a gallop. Unable to see in front, she could only suppose danger surrounded them. All her strength was concentrated on clinching to his body, her cheek pressed against his back, her eyes closed. At any moment she expected the crackle of a shot or the chaos of an attack, although she could only put her mind to just staying on the horse.

When she slipped from the rump, Cole reined in, clutching her arm to stop her from crashing to the dirt. Instead, his firm grip swung her to her feet, as he steered the horse in the opposite direction. Although shaken, Jane could see now what was so urgent. The white canvased wagon swayed in the middle of the Pecos River, tossed about by the churning waters.

While she ran there, Cole arrived at the bank, lashing the reins on the palomino's flanks to have it charge into the river. As she neared, she saw Major Perry pulling the harness of the front horses, his own mount barely able to keep its head above the water. The boat-shaped wagon floated but appeared about to tip any instant.

"Turn 'em upstream," Cole yelled at Jeffers, who was obviously overmatched by the situation. He then waved at Perry to guide the horses into the current, just as a ship would steer into the wind. The major, with only a hold on one of the horses, couldn't alter the course. Lapping waves, splashing in the faces of man and animal, added to the confusion.

With the water at her knees, Jane stopped upon realizing she too could be swept away.

Then she saw Cole, submerged to the waist, screaming and whistling, left hand full with the palomino's mane, forcing the horse past the wagon on the downstream side, whipping the team one by one with just the reins of his own mount. When he reached the front horses, he too grabbed their harness. With him at one side and Perry at the other, the two riders led the team closer to the far bank.

Within just yards of land, rider and horse slowly emerged from the river, followed by each pair of the team. The right wheels erupted through the surface. A scream within the wagon focused Jane's attention on Adela, who was thrown to the side and crashed into the inner wall. A black bundle flew over the side. An instant later, Adela's violent cries confirmed Jane's fear. It was the baby, Joaquin.

Reflex made Jane trudge deeper, but the powerful force and the soft silt mired her progress. It was then she noticed Cole again charging the palomino back into the river. Joaquin bobbed momentarily above the waves, his cries muffled by the water. He sank below the surface, but the long black shawl still trailed on the water.

As it brushed against a dead tree trunk firmly stationed in the river's center, Cole drew his knife and hurled the blade, piercing the cloth and stabbing the wood. He swung his leg over the palomino's head and jumped into the raging waters. In two strokes he was at the trunk to grasp the shawl and quickly reel it back to the surface, the end snarled around the small body.

With the reins in his right hand, he shouted at the horse, which turned about to the shore, dragging Cole and the infant he held above the waves. Once Perry led the wagon on dry land, Adela leaped from the wagon and scurried to her child. Cole knelt, putting his ear to the baby's chest. He held up Joaquin by the ankles and spanked his bottom like a newborn. Anxious seconds later, water gushed from the infant's throat and welcome cries of life filled the air.

Adela scooped up her son to squeeze him lovingly in her arms. Jane put her hand to her mouth. The thought that Joaquin might have lost his life choked her breath and brought tears to her eyes. The scene of mother and child rejoined made her sob at the outcome and the thought of what might have been. Her eyes darted to the man responsible.

Cole was still on his knees. She couldn't read his face from the distance, but he looked back at her and shook his head. Soon, he was on his horse and across the river.

"You okay?" he asked when he arrived.

She could only nod.

Without pause, he went to the burro and cart, which Jane had just noticed had been abandoned. He dismounted and in little time unhitched the animal and led it by the reins. He again eyed her, his face stern and full of purpose. Again in the saddle, he offered his familiar hand and she was behind him once more. A hand on the reins, the other leading the burro, he kicked the palomino.

Jane held him tightly as she had before. She was filled with questions, but his expression and silence kept her mouth closed. Cold water wrapped around her. It rose up to her chest, squeezing the breath nearly from her. As soon as she felt the water nearly carry her off the horse, gravity pulled her back on the rump as the palomino finished the crossing.

He steered toward the others, who had gathered around the wagon. Jeffers and Apperson huddled around Adela, showing their relief at the boy's rescue. Perry stood alone by his horse. Cole helped Jane down, then quickly was off the horse, marching straight for the major, slamming his fist into Perry's jaw, sending the officer on his back.

"What in hell did you try a fool thing like that for?" Cole shouted, drawing all eyes his way. "You nearly got them killed and me trying to save you."

Perry rubbed his jaw, not anxious to answer. He got to a knee, then thrust a punch into Cole's gut, bending Cole over. "I had no other choice." Another punch on the chin now had Cole on the ground.

Worried by the fight, Jane took a step to try and stop it, but was stopped by Apperson's grasp of her arm. "I sense this is a long time in coming, my dear. It's better not to involve yourself. I don't believe it will last long."

Climbing to his feet, Perry stood over Cole. "I didn't know where you were or if you were even alive. I had to presume you weren't, so I decided to lead these people back to civilization." He pointed to the river. "The storm had formed a sand spit. I seized the chance to cross."

With a swiping kick, Cole took out Perry's legs, grabbed the major's collar and reared back for another punch. "You risked their lives on that? You damn fool, I ought bust out what little brains you got and leave you on that spit."

Perry drew his pistol as did Cole, both of them pointed at the other's chin.

"Stop this," Jane shouted. "You're both behaving like children. Instead of attacking each other, we all should give thanks for being alive."

"No thanks to him," Cole said, staring at Perry.

"But alive none the less. To reach our goal we will need the help of everyone, and that includes you two, without the spilling of any further blood."

Cole tasted the trickle coming from his lip. The woman's speech made sense as much as he hated to admit it. He eased the hammer to rest. Perry, rolling his eyes at Jane, slowly did the same. Both men got to their feet. Without further words exchanged, they both brushed the dirt and mud from their clothes.

"Mr. Cole," said Apperson in a tone oblivious of the mood. "It was your intention to have us at the trading post by this evening. I suggest you get about your duty." The Englishman led Adela and Jeffers to the wagon, leaving Jane alone to stand and stare at him.

Cole walked by her, giving her a momentary

glare. He retrieved his hat, paused, then picked up the soaked shawl. "From now on, you ride with the wagon."

She felt dispirited at his remark, as if he blamed her for the trouble. She watched him walk away, believing what small bond she'd built with him was now shattered.

Chapter Eleven

Four framed shacks stood silhouetted by the afternoon glare. Shelter was a welcome sight. The heat had beaten the dirt into powder that swirled about in the dry breeze. Much of the party wore a pale coat of dust, including the wagon and all the horses. As Cole blinked dust from his eyes, he was reminded of Chet Burroughs's warning about the place.

He reined his horse around to the wagon. "I'm going ahead. The ranger was saying there could be some rough fellows here. One of them may be the fellow that runs the place."

Apperson eagerly nodded, apparently due to his sole interest of escaping the heat. Cole peeked into the wagon. For a instant, his eyes caught Jane's. Her face was red and dripped with sweat and she turned it upon being seen by him.

"I'm coming along," said Perry as he came beside Cole.

"No. I'll go alone."

Perry shook his head as he nudged his horse. "I don't take orders from you."

Cole spurred the palomino to catch him. Once alongside, he wasn't sure if the major wanted to finish what was started when they crossed the Pecos.

"She's an attractive woman," Perry said, staring straight ahead. Cole looked at him, puzzled.

"Yeah, I guess so. Didn't think you was the kind to make kind remarks about ladies."

"Just because I don't think this country a suitable place to bring women doesn't mean I'm blind. I've always admired beauty." He glanced at Cole then faced forward. "I also know what effect they have on men."

"How do you mean that?"

Perry sternly eyed him. "I know how they can persuade. I hope nothing occurred while the two of you were off on your own to change your mind about coming with me once this is over."

"You ought to mind your own business." Cole thought his answer might suggest something about Jane it shouldn't. "We were holed up in a hollow in the rocks waiting out the storm. That's it, that's all." In defense of her honor and his, he recalled what he learned while with Jane. "We did read the letter. The one you give me. You read it, didn't you?"

The major faced away from him. "It was my duty as a soldier to use whatever within my means to secure my objective. Just the same, I am counting on you to honor your commitment."

"I told you I would. Besides, I guess Claire Rhodes may do some good," he said softly, steering his eyes straight. The two riders came over railroad tracks, which glistened in the sun without a speck of rust. Although they had at first appeared as shacks, the structures were actually tents. The canvas covers had some age on them. Most appeared sturdy as if newly built. A small store was on the right with mostly Mexican women and children surrounding the shaded front. Across the street, four horses were tethered in front of the largest tent. It appeared to be a saloon, but Cole didn't recognize the words on the sign. He tapped Perry's arm and pointed to it.

" 'Langtry.' Little doubt what you'll find in there," said Perry. The officer dismounted and approached a Mexican youth by a cart of apricots. "How much?"

The boy held up a single finger.

"A dollar?" Perry asked surprised. "How much do the locals pay?" The boy seemed confused by the question.

"Probably only speaks Mex," said Cole, angling his left leg around the saddlehorn.

"In a rail town? I bet he knows more than he lets on." Perry held up two fingers. "I'll buy two," he said, retracting a finger, "for one dollar."

The boy beamed and nodded.

"Give him a dollar," Perry said, selecting two apricots.

"Now, who's cheating who?" Cole reluctantly drew the coin from his pocket and flipped it to the boy, who gave it a single bite, then ran to show the prize to his relatives in the shade. Perry sniffed both fruits and tossed one to Cole. As Cole sank his teeth into the apricot, the juice squirted into his tongue. The tartness puckered his cheeks, but he savored the sweet moisture before swallowing.

"You know, Cole," Perry said while chewing, "this whole affair reminds me of a campaign in Dakota Territory. We searched three days for renegades attacking miners. Eventually, we found it wasn't renegades, but rival miners attacking each other."

Cole took another bite, but his teeth ground into the pit. He engulfed it in a larger bite, bellowed his cheek and spat it to the street. "What's that got to do with this?"

"The futility. The expense of our resources chasing something that didn't exist. Somehow, I can't help but compare this situation to that."

"I know what you mean," said Cole. "I'm beginning to think the same thing. But that woman doctor, she's still convinced of it." His own words reminded him of what Jane had read in the letter. She wasn't the only female that chased after fool ideas against higher odds. In the case of Claire Rhodes, the fool idea was the belief in his own innocence. It made him reconsider that some ideas were worth driving after until they came to an end.

"You two," erupted a voice from behind. Cole faced about to see a man with a star steadying a double barrel shotgun at them both. "Real easy like, throw them pistols to the dirt."

Cole looked at Perry, who showed the same confusion at the order. When the lawman cocked both hammers, the two of them slowly complied.

"What's the meaning of this? I'm Major Miles Perry of the Army of the United States."

"I don't care if you're the ghost of Davy Crockett. It's against the law to be spitting in Langtry without a permit. Both of you shut your mouths and raise your hands. You're going to see the judge."

"Permit?" Cole asked. "For spitting out a pit? Listen friend, we got a wagon party—"

"I told you to hush your mouth and climb down off that horse."

With the weapon trained at him, Cole slowly dismounted and walked across the street. The puny lawman kept warily behind them, carefully picking up the pistols. Once under the tent's awning, they stopped at the opening. Cole didn't feel comfortable heading in without an escort. A shove in the back with the double barrel made them march inside.

The hot interior was illuminated only by the light through the canvas. An untended saloon bar made of hastily nailed planks was to the left. A round table in the middle was surrounded by four men playing cards.

"What is it, Bob?" an wrinkled dark faced white man staring at his hand asked. He had a scruffy white-peppered beard and wore an eastern derby.

"I brought these two in, Judge. I caught them spitting outside on the street. They don't have no permit, seeing as they just rode in."

The old man peeked at Cole then Perry, then back to his hand. "You really with the army, or did you steal them duds?"

"I am an officer with the Army of the United States. My name is Major Miles—"

"I didn't ask you your name," shouted the judge. "What's the army doing here? He got soldiers with him?"

"No, your honor," answered the one with the shotgun. "They was by themselves. I didn't see no soldiers."

"As I said—" Perry continued, only to be silenced by a single finger pointed at him by the judge, whose eyes were locked on his cards. He tossed two chips in the center of the table.

"I'll see you your ten dollars and I'll take two cards."

"But you've already drawn three," replied an equally gruff cardplayer across the table.

"I did that after you raised me."

"Yeah, but you can't draw any cards unless you raise."

The judge lurched over the table. "Damn you, Harold, this is my place, my table, my cards, and it's my game. Give me them two cards."

Reluctantly, the dealer complied with the judge who twitched as if stuck with a thorn once receiving them. "So, Major. You never did say what the army is doing here."

"I am here alone." answered Perry.

Cole winced at the major's honesty. It was clear he was no better cardplayer than the judge.

"Alone, huh? Well, the fine for spitting in the street without a permit is five dollars. Payable on demand." He looked at the small stack of chips in front of him. "I'll demand it now."

"Five dollars?"

"Or you can buy a permit and I'll drop the charges."

"And just how much is a permit?"

The judge smirked to his friends. "Five dollars."

A glance at Perry's reddening face told Cole he was likely in for trouble.

"You, sir, are no judge, *your honor*. You're a scalawag saloonkeeper. Certainly not the type of authority to sit in judgement of me."

"That's it!" said the judge, slamming his card hand on the table. "I find you in contempt of court. That's another ten."

"Why not double it?" Perry said defiantly.

"Sold," retorted the judge, who then smiled to his fellow players. "Twenty-five dollars. I love doing business with the army."

After a loud guffaw by all those at the table, Perry grunted his throat clear. Cole knew what he'd say, aware Perry didn't have any money and he himself had spent his last dollar on the apricots.

"I have no intention of paying you twenty-five dollars or twenty-five cents. I am going to leave this den of iniquity and shall expect no more harassment by you or your sorry bunch unless you want to face extreme consequences by the United States Army." Perry faced about and so did Cole, only to have the shotgun aimed in his face.

"Back up, friend," said Cole. "Or I'll bust that scattergun right over your head."

The puny man trembled, shaking his fingers too close to both triggers. Before he found himself shot by mistake, Cole backhanded a grip on the double-barrel tubes, wrenching it from the nervous lawman's hands, then fired a fist into the man's jaw. The scratch of chair legs scooting across the dirt floor made Cole turn. The dealer began to draw his revolver, but was stopped by the slap of the shotgun's stock against his head. The judge sat while the two remaining cardplayers rose. Perry punched one to the ground, while the other stepped on the table to leap at Cole, who caught the attacker by the collar and belt in midair and continued the flight by throwing him out the opening.

A ratchet of a hammer froze Cole still. A muzzle stabbed at the back of his head made him raise his hands. "If you even take a breath, it's adios amigo," the judge warned. Perry's eyes were wide open, making Cole think this was the end of the line.

"I say," boomed a familiar voice from the opening. Cole peeked from the corner of his eye to spot Apperson and Jane standing in the threshold. "Might I intercede on my friends' behalf?"

"Who the hell are you?" the judge demanded.

"Nigel Apperson," he said, extending his hand and walking into the tent. The judge seemed confused by the Englishman's amiable behavior. "Member of Parliament and servant to Her Majesty the queen."

"Huh? Where you come from?"

"I had just arrived outside your door, when one of these gentlemen came flying past."

"No! I meant where were you born?"

"London. Great Britain. You've heard of it, I trust?"

The slow click of the hammer being eased made Cole flinch.

The judge acted as if he had really seen the ghost of Davy Crockett. "I'll be damned. You're one of them English dandies, aren't you?"

Apperson grinned, surveying the surrounding Texans and the awe they held him in. "In the flesh."

The judge tucked the pistol in his belt and heartily accepted Apperson's outstretched hand. "Roy Bean, justice of the peace of Langtry, and damn glad to know you."

"Langtry?" Apperson noted. "I don't suppose . . . ?"

"Named for Miss Lillie herself."

"I thought it was for the rail foreman who came—."

"Damn you, Bob. Keep your mouth shut," yelled Bean, quickly changing to his tone to his honored guest. "That's Bob. Sackhead, we call him. Don't pay him no mind." He yanked a tumbled chair for Apperson to sit and then noticed Jane. He quickly removed the derby from his balding scalp and pointed at the card dealer reentering the tent. "There's a lady present. Can't you see she needs a chair, Harold?" The dealer presented a chair to her and both she and Apperson sat near the table.

Stunned at the turn of events, Cole retrieved his hat from the dust as did Perry. He, too, appeared dazed. The mood of those in the place went from combat of opposing lines to respect for a commanding general in just the blink of an eye.

"Yes, sir, I named it in her honor," Bean continued as he sat. "No finer flower than Miss Lillie ever bloomed."

"To be sure. I couldn't agree more." Apperson smiled like a politician amid his supporters. "I'm sure she would be quite impressed. I shall tell her of your tribute when I return home."

"You know Miss Lillie?"

"Intimately. She and I spoke at a gathering just after her debut performance prior to my departure." Apperson looked at Jane. "Forgive me," he said, bobbing his head between her and the judge. "May I present Miss Jane Reeves from Boston."

"Pleasure, ma'am," said Bean, then switching his attention to the dealer, who still rubbed his head. "Harold, get these folks a drink at half price." His face showed he thought the gesture generous.

"How kind," replied Apperson. "I trust I will be able to establish an account."

"Hell, yes," Bean cheerfully agreed. "I love how you people talk in our language."

"Yes, quite remarkable isn't it?" Apperson glanced at Cole and Perry. "I'm wondering if I could assist my friends in the dispute in which they find themselves?"

"They're friends of yours?"

"Yes, actually. They're employees of mine."

"Case dismissed," Bean said, slapping the table with his hand as a gavel. "Now, let's talk about Miss Lillie. You really know her? You think you could talk her into coming here?"

At first looking stunned by the suggestion, Apperson spoke as if singing a familiar tune. "Of course. I'm sure she would be delighted. She's quite attentive to her admirers. And with you being the local magistrate, naming the town after her, I'm sure she would make every effort."

"That's what I like to hear." Bean took the bottle and the shot glasses from Harold. "Let's drink to it." They both downed the quickly poured liquor in a single swig toast. After wiping his mouth with his sleeve, Bean coughed out some of the burn.

"So, Mr. Bean," said Jane. "You're the only authority there is in this area? This side of the Pecos River?"

He nodded and his expression changed to thoughtful reflection. "I kind of like the sound of that." He stretched his arms apart as an artist imagining a painting. " 'Law west of the Pecos.' Kinda' has a ring to it."

"A befitting moniker if there ever was one," Apperson remarked. "Just as Mrs. Langtry is known as 'The Jersey Lilly.'" The judge's stunned expression weakened Apperson's smile. "She was born there, you see. The island of Jersey? In the English Channel?"

Bean's blank stare appeared as if he were a deaf mute, until he slowly spoke. "She's a married woman?"

"Oh, yes, indeed. Edward Langtry, I believe is his name."

The news etched disappointment across Bean's face just like the loss of close kin. "Damn. It didn't say nothing about that next to her poster I saw in the San Antonio newspaper. Knowing that kind of takes the wind out of a fellow."

"Well, no matter. Rest assured she is quite faithful to her public. That much I can tell about her."

"Lord Apperson," said Jane. "Perhaps Judge Bean would be able to share with us his knowledge of the area."

"I don't understand."

"Our purpose for being here," she hinted.

"Oh, yes. Quite right." He faced Bean, who liberally poured himself another drink from the bottle. Distracted by the action, Apperson watched as Bean poured all those around the table a drink as well, with his being the last. Bean gave him a sly grin.

"You were saying?"

Harold shuffled the deck. The cards slapping together finally made Apperson focus on the matter at hand. "I was wondering if you might know of a certain rock?"

"Rock? Hell, yes, there thousands of them all around here. Be my guest, load up a wagonful." All those at the table laughed.

"No," Jane said over the laughter. "It should be a large stone by itself. Something unusual. Maybe in an area where it sits alone."

"Sounds like that'n that sits in the valley," said Bob.

"You know of this place? Could you take us there?" Jane's excitement made the slight man shy away from the question.

"Speak up, Sackhead." At the judge's order Bob scratched his chin in thought. "Well, you know, Judge. That big'n the size of a house about a day's ride north of here."

The card game stopped. Cole peered around. Bob's description put an ominous caution on everyone's face.

"You don't want to go there," Bean said, resuming the game.

"And why is that?" asked Jane.

" 'Cause, there's Comanches there, little lady. Been looting and burning farms and ranches. You'd be a fool to go there." He eyed his cards. "I'll open with two dollars."

"Would there be anyone here who would like to show us this place?" Apperson asked. "I would be willing to make it worth his while."

Bean cocked his eye at the Englishman. "Just how worth his while are you offering?"

"Oh. I should say one hundred dollars."

"*Hah.*" Bean looked at his cards again. "Hunerd dollars is not worth my while. Come on, Harold. It's up to you. Are you in or you out?"

"I ain't going out there for no hundred dollars."

"I meant the game, you jackass."

"I might be willin'." Bob's announcement silenced the room.

Bean looked at him with amazement as did everyone else. "Damn, Bob. Last man I thought would volunteer is you."

"Maybe you don't know me that well, Judge? A hunerd dollars is a lot a money." Bob looked to Apperson. "You got the money with you?"

"Indeed. However, I would only be willing to pay half at this time. The remainder issued after you have successfully led us there."

"Well, I'll take you out there, but like the judge says, they're Comanches out there. I ain't staying to get scalped."

"How many you reckon?" asked Cole.

"I never seen them. I just seen what they do."

The remark confirmed more than Cole wanted to hear. His better sense about this whole matter began to turn. He glanced at Jane, but she seemed unshaken by what was said. "There was a ranger who we was supposed to meet up with here. The name's Chet Burroughs."

"Old Chet was coming here?" Bean asked. "Good. He owes me money."

"I don't think so, Roy," Harold said, taking a card. "I think it's you that owe him. Ever since you drew a jack and he drew an ace."

Bean furrowed his brow, then raised his eyebrow. "Well, maybe he forgot. Anyway, he ain't been here in six months or better."

"He should've been here by now." Cole looked at Jane and Apperson. Neither showed any concern.

"He must have been delayed, Mr. Cole," Apperson said, then pointed to the slim Bob. "Mr. Sackhead's services will do."

Cole looked at Bean. "He and a fellow named Mouton were bringing in bodies of Texas Rangers that got ambushed by them Comanches two days ago."

"Is that how you say it? Moo-tawn?"

All of the party were interested at Bob's question.

Jane moved to the edge of the chair. "Why do you ask?"

"There's a trunk with that strange name on it that got dropped off by the train over a week ago."

"Where is it?" asked Cole.

"Down in the shed they keep their baggage. It's locked but the judge there, he has the key."

Bean peered back and forth between the pot and his cards.

Cole thought the trunk's presence peculiar. "I want to see it." Bean kept his eyes on his cards, wearing Cole's patience thin. "I ain't saying it again."

"Now hold on, you. That there is private property. The railroad didn't give me no key to that shed so I could give tours of it." Before Cole could answer, Apperson proposed what appealed most to the judge.

"Let us consider the possibility that I should

double the amount on the table you are playing for."

Roy Bean quickly stared the Englishman in the eye. "Cash?"

Apperson drew the bills from his coat pocket. "Of course."

Bean slammed his palm on the table again. "Sold. What are we waiting on? Let's go."

Cole, Perry, Jane and Apperson followed Bean and his deputies out of the tent. Adela and Jeffers still sat in the wagon. They were motioned to follow by Apperson. The walk through the dusty street took them past three more tents, one of which appeared to be a dry-goods merchant. Scattered debris of bent spikes and empty whiskey bottles served as reminders of the recent railroad expansion. As they neared the tracks, a small wood-plank shack little bigger than an outhouse stood alone. A latch over the door was bolted over and padlocked shut.

Bean fumbled with several keys for a moment, until he matched the correct one with the lock. With the door finally opened, a large chest sat in the middle of the shack, surrounded by lanterns and shovels. Cole and Perry drug it out into the light. The name brush painted on the top was SERGE MOUTON.

"What do you suppose he would send out here?" asked Perry.

Cole shook his head. "Don't make no sense to me."

"It could be anything," said Jane. "They

could be his private things. It might be his intention to settle here."

All the men eyed one another to see if any of them agreed with her. None showed signs of doing so. "I say we find out," Cole said. He drew the Colt and cocked the hammer. The shot split the shackle. Once open, the truck revealed shirts, pants, boots, coats, paper with writing not in English and other small items of wardrobe.

"You see," Jane said with spite. "Nothing to be concerned over. Now, you've invaded the man's privacy." She glared at the men who had thought her idea of Mouton settling here silly, especially Cole.

"It still don't make sense. Why would he send all his clothes out here? I ain't believing he plans to live here."

"No. Not here. Del Rio."

Again, all eyes went to Bob, who once more appeared embarrassed at the attention.

"Spit it all out at one time, Bob," chided Bean.

"The railroad man said this freight was bound for Del Rio. But the track had to be fixed. They didn't want to be holding on to it, 'cause once the track got fixed, they was behind and moving straight through."

Cole looked to Perry. "Do you suppose they might have went there first?"

The major shook his head. "Just so they could drag a trunk back with them?"

"No matter," Apperson said, then turning to Bean. "Your honor, I should like to stand good for this trunk. I'll have it loaded in our wagon, and when we meet our friend, I shall give it to him there."

"Sounds good to me. I don't like be in charge of it anyhow." He took the money from Apperson's hand. "I say we go back and make good use of this." They both smiled and all but Cole and Perry turned about to return to the bar.

"Hey, you, Bob," Cole firmly called, bringing the slim deputy back to him. "I'll want to leave early in the morning to find Captain Burroughs and Mouton."

"What about the stone?" asked Jane.

"No," said Cole. "I want to find them first. You stay here with the two old men and the girl. You'll be safe. Major Perry and I will search for them at first light."

"Absolutely not!" Her eyes were wide with fire. "I can't stay here for who knows how long. Time is of the essence."

"How come?"

The anger faded from her face. "I'm not able to say right now." She glanced at Bob.

Cole let out a huff. "We ain't takin' no wagon. We'll have to ride quick, and you can't be riding in no skirt. It's best if you stay here."

She peeked at her clothes. "I'll find something else." She put her hands on her hips. "You'll have to trust me, Mr. Cole. It is imperative that I find the stone as soon as possible. Our mission depends on it."

Chapter Twelve

Dawn had long passed, but Cole, Perry and Jane had barely traveled out of sight of Langtry. Most of the delay couldn't be blamed on Sackhead Bob's timid lead, but rather the late start caused by the woman doctor. Her insistence of innocence little surprised Cole. Now, as he rode over the rocky terrain, he glanced her way. Without a hat, the morning sun had already broke a sweat on her brow. His eyes wandered onto the rest of her clothes.

A man's muslin shirt replaced her stiff collar blouse. Her flushed cheeks weren't just a result of the heat and thick cloth, but due to being without benefit of the wagon-canvas shade. Long sleeves kept the sun off her arms and the size was the only one to cover her bust and still button shut. It was a simpler choice than her dungarees. A glimpse at the dirt showed the reason he demanded she wear them.

The mule she rode on Bean's rent of two dollars a day strode through the thick prickly pear cactus, which most horses avoided. Her legs dangled close to the thorns. Cole knew they wouldn't have gotten far if her skirt had become easily snagged. Pants made for the waist of a boy but with the length of a average man were difficult to find. Boots covered her bare ankles, but she complained of needing to curl her toes so they wouldn't slip off her feet.

The only solution to solve all concerns were cowhide chaps. The strap fastened to the chap wrapped around the boot's sole and would secure each to the other. As luck would have it, the single pair in Langtry belonged to Bean. A onetime price of fifteen dollars was bargained, as long as they were returned. No hat could be found in the camp with a brim that didn't sink below her eyes, despite Bean's effort to find one. No bigger gold mine had ever been found in Langtry to equal Apperson's expense to outfit Jane Reeves for travel. Cole thought they could be on their way only an hour after daybreak.

Once dressed in her new duds, Jane was ready to climb atop the mule. She hesitated, then excused herself. Cole figured she had to take care of her nature once Adela was called for behind one of the tents. When the Mexican girl ran to the men and stuttered in her chopped English for Cole's help, he first thought they had seen a snake. He ran around the tent, ready to draw iron only to find Jane wrestling with a snarled knot, her face a mixture of flustered strain.

Cole quickly slipped the knots loose which slackened the chaps from the pants and was then shooed away. Minutes later, he was called once more to tie the hank knots around her inseam, which she had attempted and failed. The tangle took time to fix, so he knelt to get a better look. Her jittery stance as he bound the leather straps was steadied when she gripped his shoulders. When he finished he noticed his nose was level with her hips. He looked up into her eyes. Their movement from the position served as a mutual agreement not to mention what happened to the others.

To save her embarrassment, he told the others he'd killed a snake. Unaware of his lie when she arrived, she salvaged her pride with a bigger lie about him taking up time alone behind the tents for his own causes. Scattered chuckles left the men with the idea Cole had trouble holding his own water. Soon after they left Langtry, he reined the palomino down a slope and glanced to her to catch what he thought was an appreciative grin for his discretion.

He now looked back to see the tent city gone below the horizon, and realized he could survive the humiliation among men better than she.

"I think we should head further north to find Burroughs and Mouton," Perry said.

A squint at the sun overhead prompted Cole to agree. "That might be best. We'll need to be on their trail before sundown."

"But," Jane blurted, "what if they're going to Langtry in another direction? We'll spend valuable time looking for them."

"We can't know that." Cole spurred the palomino to catch Bob. "How far to this valley?"

"Three miles, maybe four from here." Bob's answer only fueled Jane's excitement.

"You see. It wouldn't be prudent to travel so far when one of our objectives is so close."

"Why is it so important, Doctor?" Perry's question drew her eyes to him. "Why is it that getting there is more important than two men's lives?"

She hesitated, first looking at Bob, then Perry and finally Cole. It was clear she wasn't comfortable answering while the lawman or the officer were present.

"Maybe it would suit everybody if we split up." Cole pointed to Perry. "The major and I can scout for the ranger and Mouton." He looked to Jane. "You and Bob can go find this stone you need to see so bad."

"*No!*" Jane's loud rejection made apparent her discomfort of being alone with Bob. Her eyes wide like those of a child being left by a parent confirmed it, but a second later, she relaxed them just enough to not be rude. Without a word said, Cole knew that he was the only one with whom she would feel safe being alone. There was no sense in arguing.

"Why don't you gone on ahead," Cole said to Bob. The slim lawman rode further away, but the other three reined in.

Perry eyed Cole with disappointment at the

submission to the woman's wishes. "What do we do now?"

A pause between the trio gave Cole time to think of a plan. "Scout for signs of them two till near sundown. If you find them, fire a shot. If I hear more than one, I'll take it you need help and we'll come ridin'. If you find neither, we'll meet you back in Langtry."

"What about him?" Perry said, motioning at Bob.

"We'll need him to lead us to this rock we're looking for."

Perry's drawn cheeks showed he didn't think much of the idea. After a few moments, he took a long breath and let it out, straightened his hat and turned his roan to the north. "Good luck, you two. I believe you'll need it."

With the major out of earshot, Cole looked to the woman doctor. Jane appeared reluctant to speak, but after several silent moments, she seemed to summon the confidence to explain. Cole nudged the palomino and she had the mule follow.

"Cortés's letter tells of a certain time when the chamber reveals what is inside. It isn't specific, likely to mask the details from those he feared would take the treasure, or perhaps he himself is unsure. I don't know which. Nevertheless, it suggests that the chamber can only be accessed at a particular time. There are references to the sun. As if something about it determines when the chamber can be opened."

"Yeah? So what does that have to do with this all-fire hurry?"

"I don't know. That's what worries me. It's intuition really; I have nothing else to rely on. But I can't keep from believing that we have only a limited time to find what we seek."

"So you're just guessing about all this?"

"Not all this. Everything I've told you is the truth. It's just the enigma of the sun reference. I don't know what it means yet, but I'm confident the answer lies with the stone."

Cole shook his head and out of the corner of his eye he spotted Bob, who had reined his horse to a stop while staring at the ground. When Cole came along side, he saw what it was that stopped the slim man. Dismounting the palomino, he knelt on the sand and pulled the arrow from the ground. The charred tip snapped easily. He had seen the marks on the tail before.

"Comanche," he muttered.

"Yeah," said Bob. "And when they set fire to it and shoot it in the air, it's to serve as a boundary not to be crossed. Just like a barbed wire fence. Anybody trespasses gets scalped."

Cole peeked at Jane and nodded, reaffirming the danger. Although she swallowed hard, she didn't show any fear at the threat.

"That there's a warning I plan to heed." Bob turned his horse back to the east. Jane watched him as he rode past her.

"What about the valley? Where is it? Where do we go?"

"You're heading straight for it. Just keeping riding and you'll end up there or in Hell, one or the other."

Cole chuckled in silence. The thought occurred to him that maybe Bob wasn't such a sackhead after all. With one look at the woman doctor and the resolve in her face to go on, Cole felt more like he was suited for a burlap hat if he went further. He put the blackened arrowhead in his shirt pocket. "He's right, you know."

"Now you? Are you going to join him? Because if you are, I plan to go right on without you."

He rose and stood beside her horse. She arched her shoulders in defiant determination. It would be easy to climb onto the palomino and ride back with Bob, or even tie her to the saddle and take her too, if it weren't for the nagging he'd have to hear. There was another idea. The same one she held. If he got her to where she wanted to go and back without any holes in him or her, then he would have done his job. He looked into her eyes. "There's a fair chance we'll get killed."

Without as much as a dent in her expression she answered, "Clay, this is the chance of a lifetime. If I let it slip away, then I won't have a life with which to worry. I've got to go."

He took a moment to think of what lay ahead before mounting the palomino. His horse jerked with his kick but Cole held it to an amble so as not to outstride the mule. It wasn't long before she came alongside him. "Thank you," she said.

"Don't thank me yet," he grumbled. "I promised a long time ago I wouldn't die in Texas.

184

And if I come to doing just that, you better hope the same for you or I'll haunt you for the rest of your days."

A crack of a smile showed she wasn't frightened by his mock threat. As her smile increased, he felt one crease his face. "Well, not that I look forward to either fate," she said. "What is it about Texas that you fear losing your life?"

The question made him take a deep breath. Memories flooded his mind. At first, he penned them inside as he always did, but a second thought had him consider the good it might do him to let them loose. He exhaled with a rush from his billowed cheeks.

"My pa was killed in Texas. He's buried not far from where the Rio Grande flows into the Gulf of Mexico. A place named Palmito Ranch."

He turned to Jane, her mouth open, her eyes wide and brows raised. Her face took a somber expression, but he wasn't looking for pity.

"As it turned out, the war had been over for near a month since Lee offered his sword to General Grant. So in May of '65 our outfit was ordered to put an end to Confederate shipping from the gulf. The War Department figured they had put out the big fire at Appomattox and didn't want any embers to spark into bigger ones and cause more bloodshed. My pa was a captain for the Sixty-second colored troops that was formed in Missouri commanded by Lieutenant Colonel Branson. He didn't take to the idea at first. Most officers didn't think much about leading black soldiers. But General Grant knew my pa and asked him, rather than plain ordering him to. My Pa told me later that he had never felt more proud of any men than he did of them." Cole looked ahead, but he still felt her eyes on him.

With another long breath, he recalled the details he'd tried to forget most of his life. "I was nearing sixteen, so they let me give up the drum I had beat all during the war and carry a musket. Some said it weren't right to put a white boy amongst the colored, but I didn't care. I had drummed for the lines for my pa since my ma died back in '61. The troopers weren't any different than whites, and I come to know them pretty good, although my pa told me to hang near the rear to stay clear of the fighting as much as I could."

The fond memory made him smile, but his face tightened as he recalled the events of the final two days. "I remember it was raining hard. A storm had blown in and we marched in mud near knee-deep. The superior officer in charge was Colonel Barrett and he had joined us up with a white regiment, the Thirty-fourth Indiana. We were all led by cavalry on our way to Brownsville, where the cotton was being shipped from. The first reports came that the rebels had pinned down the cavalry. I could hear the fire of different skirmishes all around. We was called up from the rear to support the Thirty-fourth, but they didn't take a liking to being helped by the blacks. A bunch of squabbling commenced over who was supposed to lead, and while the different company commanders quarreled, news came that the rebs had flanked around our right and had about surrounded our rear to cut off a retreat. The Rio Grande was at our left and the rebs were every place else. The rain stopped but the clouds still hung low. There wasn't much light. I remember firing when the command came, but the dim light made it hard to see what you were shooting at, and when night came it was all you could do not to hit your own men.

"The next day, the Thirty-fourth came running from Palmito Hill and they crashed into our lines, setting off a lot of confusion. The retreat order had been passed on. Our company was ordered to shield the rear from the rebs. Talk was we were picked to die, and the gloom of the clouds and the spatter of few raindrops made it seem true. That was the time I was most scared. Soon, we were left on our own. Some of the troopers of Company G wanted to run rather than be captured by white Confederates. Word was they shot black captives. Through all the yelling, I remember my pa's shout for them to keep their heads. All went quiet listening to him. He told them to be proud they were soldiers, fighting not just for their own kind, but for the Union, for *their* country. It may be the last time to prove themselves as good as any white troop, he told them. And how he was honored to be their commander. After that, there was no more talk of desertion, just fighting. We repelled every reb charge. The smoke was so thick it was hard to breathe, much less see. But we held the line, and the rebs stopped coming."

Cole dipped his head for a moment, but he had made up his mind to tell the whole story. He glanced at Jane, whose eyes were still firmly locked on him despite the sweat dripping from her red cheeks. Never at ease being stared at, he again looked forward.

"Along about sundown came the order to fire. We had massed at the rear, and Colonel Branson figured we couldn't get back to where we landed. I looked to my pa, who was mounted next to Branson. When the colonel ordered to cease fire, he turned to my pa, Captain Robert Cole, and said, 'That winds up the war.' My pa looked at me and gave me a grin, as if relieved I was still alive." Hesitant to continue, Cole forced the words from his swelled throat.

"And then, I heard a single crack in the air, a shot. I jerked around to see if the rebs were charging, but none came and there was no more shooting. I looked back at my pa. His grin was pained, then I saw the blood staining his gut. He slumped from his horse to the ground. I ran to him, but he couldn't speak as blood streamed from his mouth. My eyes welled up with tears, and he wiped them from my cheeks. He never liked to see me cry. Then his hand sagged to the dirt. The officers pulled me away from him to let the surgeon get to him. They had to drag me away. I was yellin' loud at him not to die."

Cole paused and swallowed hard to rid the

lump from his throat. "Branson talked to the reb colonel, and they kept him in their field hospital. It took him two days to die. Meanwhile, it was explained to the Confederates that Lee had surrendered. The war was already over. Once they were convinced, they surrendered to us, even though we were licked. Pa never liked coming to Texas, still they buried him there among the few that fell that day. It was then and there, I made him a promise while over his grave, I wouldn't be resting in Texas soil. I figured I owed him that."

"What a terrible experience," said Jane. "Especially for someone so young. I am so sorry. Please forgive my asking."

Cole shook his head. An apology wasn't needed. The heavy weight that had lodged in his gut for more than sixteen years was gone. He glanced a slight smile at her for only an instant because of the distraction before him.

A wide canyon revealed its depth with each step of the horses. He pulled up at the edge of what became a plateau. With a quick estimate he gauged 100 feet between them and the valley floor with scattered red escarpments of similar height on the other side more than a mile away. Brush pockmarked the white sand. In the center of it all stood a single boulder of such size it was clearly visible from their vantage point. Cole blinked twice, guessing ten men could stand one atop the other before they'd equal the apex.

"That's it." Jane's awe of the sight didn't deter her gaze for several seconds as if entranced. "My God, it's really there."

"What'd you expect?" he said and dismounted. "It's what you came looking for."

She quickly slipped off the mule. "Yes, but it's exactly like I imagined. It's breathtaking seeing something that you've thought about, dreamed about for so long."

Cole put a knee to the dirt and tossed pebbles down the side of the bluff. As it bounced further down, the crackle of each impact declined steadily until silent. The distance to the bottom was every bit as far as he had first thought and then some. "There's no getting horses down this slope."

"We'll just have to climb down," she said casually.

A slow twist gave him time to civilize his reply. "Climb down? This ain't no gentle hill. Them jagged rocks will break us to pieces if we miss one step."

"Oh, I'm sure they would." Her voice showed no concern.

"And that don't make you think twice about it, do it?"

"Not in the least."

After considerable thought on his part, he shook his head and let out a long breath. He hadn't figured the task would be easy when he started the day and wouldn't have minded a bit if proved wrong. Still, they had traveled almost the entire day, and once he took another look, he weighed how close they were to their goal. In another couple of hours, he could be headed home.

He inhaled, pondering further options, when

the arrowhead's presence in his shirt pocket forced another thought to mind. "Them Comanches could be looking at us right now. If we tried getting down there, we'd have to do it in the dark. The moon was full last night, and without any clouds we'd be easy to spot."

"What if we cloaked ourselves?"

"In what?"

"Oh," she said with a slight pause, looking at the horses. "I see what you mean." Despite pursed lips, optimism laced her mood and manner. "Well, we'll have to give it our best."

"Staying alive," he said with spite, "with traversing these rocks, in the dark, with Comanches out there, will *be* our best."

Chapter Thirteen

The moon appeared as an orange ball as it edged over the horizon at dusk. Jane watched Cole tie a rope around a large protruding rock, testing the knot's strength with firm tugs. "It's time to move," he said, tossing the rope end down the side of the bluff.

Fearful to lean over the ledge, Jane stood, curious as to the cord's length and the distance below. "Are you sure we'll make it?"

He walked to the palomino and put his hat on the horn. "Nope." The casual answer came as a shock, until he paused and faced her. "I ain't sure of nothing until we get to the bottom. This will get us far enough to stand on some rocks I saw. It starts to angle out and I reckon we can climb down from there. As long as we can see. It's getting back up that I ain't looking forward to."

The idea seemed reckless, but it was the lone option available. Jane took a breath in an effort to calm her nerves, but it did little. He slowly backed over the edge. The twine groaned as it assumed the weight, yet the knotted loop didn't yield.

With an outstretched hand he summoned her. She cautiously wrapped her arm around his neck and quickly swung her legs over his back to dig her heels into his hips. An instant later, she was relieved to her delight they weren't falling. "This isn't so bad."

Muttered gurgles came from his mouth. "I . . . can't . . . breathe."

With the realization she was killing him, sealing her own doom if she continued, she gradually eased the tension from his throat. Gravity took advantage of each slip of her grasp. She closed her eyes with his words.

"Hang on to my shoulders."

Air rushed past, brushing her cheeks and the back of her neck. A jolt stopped her, almost flinging her from his shoulders. She squeezed and squinted even tighter when Cole climbed backward. With each twist of his shoulders and hips, Jane was certain she, if not both of them, would crash onto the rocks. A final jolt convinced her she was still alive and they'd stopped moving. Relaxing her arms and extending her legs, she regained a precarious foothold.

Opening her eyes, the first surprise was the increasing gloom. Expressing gratitude for surviving seemed out of place and too costly as light seeped away each second. Without a moment lost, he took her hand and descended atop the uneven rocks jutting from the bluff.

Her misstep sent a gravel stream down the side. The sizzling sound brought Cole to glare at her. "I can't see," she said as an excuse.

He put a finger to his lips. "Keep your voice down and take more care. Now is the best time to move before that moon gets full bright."

She followed his lead, careful to place her foot and take another step down before he pulled her further. Upon reaching the rubble of large fallen stones, they were walking on more solid footing of piled dirt, rock and sand that nature has worn from the canyon wall into a gradual grade. Their walk turned to a full-stride run down the sharp angle. The leather chaps swiped against each other. She feared making more noise, so she bowed her legs only to lose her balance, fall and roll, stopping only when she reached level ground.

"Are you hurt?" he asked.

She tried to make out his face in the dim light. "I'm fine," she answered, suppressing her pain, anger and embarrassment. When he stood, she saw his silhouetted figure draw his pistol. There on her knees, her heart beat a bit quicker. For an instant she was unsure what he planned to do with it.

"Let's get this over with as quick as we can.

Stay right behind me. If you hear or see anything, poke me. If there's any firing, keep your head down."

Again, she took another calming breath and felt him take her wrist. Together they crept hunched to their knees from bush to bush. The moon had climbed higher in the sky, becoming more of a white beacon illuminating the sand of the valley floor. After several silent starts and stops, they entered the shadow cast by the towering stone.

Attempting to catch her breath from the run and the excitement, she slowly stepped to the stone. Her fingers searched the cragged granite. Unable to see anything in the shadow, she stepped from it into the moonlight. With each step, she scanned up and down, staring into the penumbrae of wind-shaved edges, yet unable to see beneath them. Walking a further around the stone brought her to the fully illuminated front.

Exploring its texture, her fingertips read the stone as the blind did Braille. Layers of disturbed sand sifted away with her touch. Rounded and sharp edges became exposed after centuries of driving wind. She continued until her thumb slipped into a elliptical depression. She brushed and dug away more sand to find it was larger than she had first thought. Frenzied with anticipation, she swiped the area as one would a window.

"What are you doing?" whispered Cole as he came next to her.

"I think I've found something."

"Do it more quiet or something will find us."

Unconcerned, Jane continued wiping until the depression became an eye, and then there was a nose. Soon emerged a face in profile, but the moonlight vanished. She twisted about to see the clouds drifting in front of the moon. If unable to see the marking, she couldn't interpret its meaning. Even with her hands on it, it was so far away. A moment later, the clouds went on with their night's flight and the stone was illuminated again.

Sculpted in relief, the figure appeared adorned with a headdress of a warrior or a member of royalty. Pecking with her nails to scrape away the dirt shroud revealed elaborate carvings around the body. Reptiles and small mammals surrounded it, but lessons on the culture reminded her these weren't mere symbols of benevolence but rather numerals.

"Are you done?"

Again trying to ignore his impatience, she concentrated on the symbols until his persistent question made it impossible. "No, I've just begun." Her fingers slipped off a raised outer edge. Once she found the spot again, she was able to wrap the heel of her hand around it. She ran her hand up the curved arch, plowing off more sand until the perimeter extended higher than her reach. "It's a circle. Like that of a calendar. Suggesting a certain time."

"Like when we should leave?"

"Be quiet," she demanded. "I need to think. The Aztecs often recorded their history in calendars. It will take time to decipher when this was."

"Jane, we ain't got time. Finish up what you're after and let's get back to the rocks."

"It's not that simple. I can't just read this like a newspaper. These symbols have meanings. It's important I recognize each one. Without putting them in proper order, it would be impossible to make sense of it." She proceeded to examine the sculpture. The center figure was pictured standing with his view directed at an angle, just as one would look upon the sky. When she found the object in line with its view, the answer popped into her head simultaneously with Cole's pointed finger and inquiry.

"What's that mean?"

"It's a skull."

"I see that. What's it mean?"

"Skulls are an important part of their beliefs. It could represent a reminder of the dead. Spirits of the sacrificed." She paused when another revelation occurred. "Or that of a deity."

"A what?"

"A god." The light faded once more. Jane kept staring at the skull, contemplating its implication, only to be awoken by Cole's grip of her arm.

"Did you hear that?" he whispered.

"What?" The light returned.

"Something's moving. We got to leave." He pulled her arm to lead her away. At the top of the calendar, she caught sight of another carving, like that of a blooming flower. The shadows made it hard to see, so she tore from his grip to take another look. Flowers weren't a predominant fixation of the Aztec, but as she focused harder in the dim light, she recognized what she thought were petals were actually rays. Rays of the sun.

"We got to leave now."

"Not yet," she gritted. Her mind was torn in two directions. Cole's warning should be heeded, however, she had learned nothing from the carving. She was close to the objective, if only she could record what she'd found. Without pen or paper, she realized another solution. It was the only one. "Give me your knife."

"What for?"

"Just give it to me. Please!"

Cole handed her the knife. Quickly she unbuttoned the muslin shirt and pulled the end of her white bodice from her pants.

"What are you doing? This ain't no time—."

"Please, just give me the arrow tip. The one that was burnt. And turn your head if you don't mind." She stuck the blade point into the garment to slice through the seam which ran below her bust to the ribs on each side. Cutting through both side seams produced a piece of cloth. Parchment. "Give me the arrow."

As he did so with one hand, she noticed the pistol in his other, a reminder she hadn't much time. She ran her fingers along the figure's line of sight. She felt an intertwined carving, but she couldn't see it clearly. "I need more light, a fire to see."

"We ain't lightin' no matches."

"Just do it. Or I'll scream." Her threat brought an angered appearance from him. For a moment, she feared he'd leave her, but was reassured when he groped through his pocket. He gave her the arrow. She snapped off the flint point and then draped the cloth over the intertwined carving. "I'll only need to see enough until I can trace it."

"It don't matter. We're probably dead anyway." He holstered the gun and cupped one hand around the other. "On the count of three. One."

She took a deep breath.

"Two."

She readied the charred stick over the cloth.

"Three."

The match flared, lighting the sculpture. Shadows grew and shrank as the flame licked the wooden match. Frantically she scrawled the charred wood on the white cloth. A carbon image emerged with each stroke. The sun was positioned over curved entwined lines, which were next to the skull.

"Hurry," he grumbled. The fire neared his fingers.

"Just a little more." The faster she rubbed the stick, the less the image materialized. "There's something else here, but it won't come through." The engraving she sought was recessed deeper than the others, eroded to a point it couldn't be copied. Jane glanced at the figure, which was too big for the cloth. Then she realized what it depicted. Distance. "This is a map," she uttered.

Cole blew the dwindling flame out and spit on his fingers.

"Let's get out of here." They crept around the rock only a short way, but she jerked from his grasp, wanting to return.

"There is a measurement there. I must find it."

"We're gettin' the Hell out of here."

"No. You don't understand. The figure was a deity. These twirled lines might indicate a presence. Perhaps Tezcatlipoca, the god of sorcery, of dead spirits. It could be a warning."

"We're amongst the Comanche. I ain't frettin' no ghosts."

She considered his logic. It pained her to leave, but perhaps they could return. She relented and went with him through the stone's shadow, resuming the crouched scamper from bush to bush, all the while imagining what she'd seen. Once at a small withered tree, Cole abruptly stopped. He pulled her in front of him and forced her to her knees. Confused, she looked up at him, but the full moon was first to catch her eye. Staring at it, suddenly the message was very clear.

"The solstice. It must be."

"Hush," he ordered while scanning behind them.

"I'm sorry. It's just that I'm now certain the summer solstice plays a part. It makes perfect sense; the position of the sun makes the chamber open. We must hurry; it's only a few days away."

"We ain't going nowhere."

His ominous tone had her lose focus on the image. "What do you mean?" Long silent seconds increased her heartbeat.

"They're hunting us."

"Who?" she blurted. He slapped his palm over her mouth, then drew the pistol again. Her heart pounded.

"They're out there, sniffing around like hounds."

He released his hand from her mouth. "Where? Who?" She arched up to peek between the tree branches but all she could see was the moonlit plain. "I don't see anything."

"Comanches are real quiet. Just look in one place, near the stone. And then you'll see them."

Although shaking, she tried to concentrate where he'd said. A hushed calm ruled the landscape. Still, she only saw the dark blotches of shaded brush. At first, she thought Cole was being overly cautious, until one of the blotches moved.

Her throat tightened, unable to utter a sound. Her trembling hand pushed a dangling twig from her view. When the shadowy presence stopped, another began in an alternate direction, sweeping around to the side. It was a maneuver she seen in the wild, as predators stalk prey. "I see two of them," she said in a wavering voice.

"I count five," he whispered. He leaned closer to her ear. "We're in it now. You got to move to them rocks before they get in front of us."

"Me? What about you?"

"Do as I say. They want both of us, but they might settle for one. When them clouds cover the moon, you run as fast you can toward the rocks and hide and don't make a sound. Run fast, you hear? Don't stop. And don't look back, no matter what happens."

"I don't know if I can do this."

"You ain't got a choice. Get ready." He drew the bowie knife and cocked the hammer of the Colt.

Unable to control her nerves, she gazed at the moon, which appeared to be dancing in the sky due to her shaking. She clutched the sketched cloth. Careful of each motion, she crouched on her toes. Two adjoined clouds floated on a course to block the moonlight. She took a shivering breath and prepared to sprint in the vague distance.

Why couldn't she have left when he told her to? Her throat was dry, so she swallowed, but it was like gulping an apple whole. If only she hadn't been so stubborn, perhaps they would have escaped before these marauders arrived.

She glanced over her shoulder at darkness encroaching like a veil. In the corner of her eye, she saw Cole keeping a steady guard. Not only had she endangered her life, it was likely she would not see him again. The thought disturbed her so, tears blurred her eyes. She pushed the regret out of her mind, to concentrate on the rocks where she had to go and nothing else.

The light faded once more. Cole shoved her as a signal to run. She charged forward. The heavy chaps slapping together impaired her stride, but she couldn't allow herself to slow her pace. Thorns and twigs scraped the leather and her skin. The pain was minimal. She couldn't afford to stop.

The light increased slightly. Darting through and around other small trees, she feared the obstacles detoured her course from the rocks too much. The unseen might trip her feet. Even though only having to run a short way, she felt a cramp grow in her ribs. If she didn't slow, she might collapse. A moving dark figure from the side made her only run faster.

The figure took shape as a human, a man with long hair. He leaped over the small brush and was just feet away from her. Instinct told her to cower and scream. An explosion rippled the air. The attacker collapsed into the darker cover of the brush. In an instant she thought it was an attempt to trip her legs, but she continued her flight with Cole's shout.

"Keep running!"

The shock of another gunshot made her stumble forward. She fought to keep her balance. Cole's voice echoed again, but she couldn't understand what he said. He'd told her not to stop; the message must be the same. Another shot made her flinch. She quivered, hardly able to keep her focus, fighting the urge to stop and sob away her terror. Footsteps thrashing through brush made her shriek and churn her legs harder. She heard heavy breathing. Could it be Cole chasing her? How could she know? If she slowed to peek over her shoulder it would cost her life. She expelled a howl and ran through the brush to the brink of fainting from fatigue. The ground vanished beneath her feet, sending her crashing into a dusty streambed. A blast rung out. A body fell on top of her. She screamed and clawed to escape, but it didn't resist. Frozen for a moment, she felt the warmth of something on her stomach. She touched it and saw her hand was covered with a dark fluid. Blood. This man was dead. A jostle of her shoulder removed the weight. She gained her feet and ran down an arroyo. The horrific sight played in her mind, but she shook her head to clear it. A large mound stood in silhouette. A rocky hill. She was close.

She trudged up a slight embankment. Her foot slipped, putting her on her knees. It was too steep to run out from, so she pawed the dirt to get to the top of the bank. She struggled up, propping her elbow over the edge as a lever to a catapult, and jumped. Her waist landed atop the edge, but the progress was too slow. Any instant she would be seized by a savage. She kicked the bank, churning her legs as if climbing a ladder, and soon was on top of the arroyo's ledge.

Her mouth agape, bellowing air in and out, she forced it closed and tried to inhale through her nose enough to satisfy her aching body. Soon she was at the rocky hill. Without sufficient cover from the small rocks, she crept as quickly as she could to find a large one to hide behind.

Upon finding a large extension of the rock to shield her from sight, she crouched behind it and closed her eyes. Struggling to maintain composure, she gave in to a momentary cry as the entire encounter raced through her mind. After clearing her eyes and nose, she noticed the silence. No more gunshots had been fired. She felt frightfully alone.

What if Cole had been killed, or worse wounded and now lay in an agonizing pain? What would she do to help him? What could she do? What was she to do for her own sake? Where could she go? Once regaining a regular breath, she peeked above the rock. Nothing moved, just as before when she knelt next to Cole beneath the tree. Surely the Comanches hadn't given up on her. However, she recalled Cole had suggested they may take him alone. She had heard stories of torture by Indians, and she again tried to conjure more positive thoughts.

The idea of seeking help shot into her mind. Carefully, she rose behind the cover of the rock and crept to the rear, keeping an eye in front of her. Returning the way they had descended to the valley was out of the question. The vast ancient flood plain seemed to stretch for miles. Miles? Major Perry! She could attempt to find him.

As she took one cautious step and then another, her idea of sneaking away vaporized with the sound of a rustle from behind. Something was again at her back. She fled, but a solid form on the ground impeded her gait, snaring her feet, sending her face first to the dirt. When she kicked, it rolled over. She recognized the form of a man, then a mustache.

She'd seen the thick light hair before. A nearby hat was familiar, too. The glinting figure of a star. A badge. The ranger Chet Burroughs! A scream at the corpse brought a crashing blow to her head.

Miles Perry lashed the roan's flanks, one hand on the reins, the other gripping the pistol. Three gunshots echoed in the dark. The full moon allowed enough light to navigate through the night. No doubt Cole and the woman were in trouble. To what degree was unknown, so he prepared for battle.

He followed the shots as best as he could guess, but it took him in another direction from where he last left them. Canyon walls stood like dark mountains. A large valley lay between them. He slowed the horse, confident he was near the source of the sound, but unsure what awaited him.

Dried brush crackled as he passed. Approaching a mound of rocks, he pointed the revolver in front, ready to fire at anything that moved. As he came around the mound, a figure lay motionless on the ground. It appeared to be a man, but he didn't relax. He knew the tricks of the savage.

Perry dismounted and slowly approached, one wary step in front of the other. Once over the figure, he recognized the clothes as that of a white man, wearing a striped coat and the trousers with the same pattern. He knelt and poked the body with the muzzle. It still didn't move and a rancid smell made clear the body had been here for days. Once he got a good look at the face, he knew it was Burroughs, the Texas Ranger, likely ambushed by Comanches.

A white cloth lay near the body. Holding it up to the light, he noticed an unusual marking and two small spots of fresh blood on the lace end. Footprints in the sand led farther into the valley.

Chapter Fourteen

Jane awoke to a blinding pain throbbing her scalp. When she tried to rub it, she found she couldn't move her hands. It took a few more moments to focus on her surroundings. Branches of a tree were above and her arms felt as if they were bound to its trunk. She peered forward to see she sat in a camp with a fire in the center. The blurred figures slowly came into clear view. Dark-skinned men squatted around the fire, laughing at her. She pressed her back against the trunk.

They wore ragged shirts and trousers more familiar to white men. Some of them had bands of cloth wrapped around the foreheads. Others let their black hair hang in their faces. Few showed a full set of teeth when they laughed.

Unsure what amused them, she first thought something had happened while she was unconscious. She panicked peeking at her still-open shirt. If they'd had their way, nothing in her body sensed it. She peeked to her pants and the chaps were still in place. The worst had not been done, yet. Her heart raced when she considered what they might have planned. Since they delighted in her fear, she tried to steady her breathing by trying to establish where she was.

Small white stones encircled the fire, almost as if in a ritual. Horrible stories came to mind in which people had been put upon flames to burn to death. If that was in store, she prayed to die first from heart failure. Further dreadful thoughts faded upon the approach of horses and a rustle from the brush.

A lighter-skinned man paraded through the camp gleaming a wide smile with a lofted hand to the Indians. He wore black pants and coat and white shirt. "Muchachos," he said in greeting. Two other men followed with belts looped with bullets across their chest. He slowly brought his attention to Jane. He furrowed his brow, then looked to the Indians. "*Quien es este mujer?*"

"*Me llamo* Jane Reeves."

He walked to her with a raised eye of disdain. "You are American?"

"Yes," she said, hopeful he would assist her. "I was kidnapped and brought here. Please help me."

He cackled, which was joined by all those in camp. "Help you? Why should I do that?"

Suddenly it was clear he was not there to save her. "Who are you?"

"I am Francisco Gura."

"Gura?" The pit of her stomach ached with the word. She closed her eyes, recalling what Chet Burroughs had said about this man. "What do you want with me?"

He glanced at the Indians, then back at her. "They brought you here because they thought you were someone else. Where is Adela?"

"Adela? Why do you want her? She's just a young girl."

"You ask too many questions for someone tied to a tree. But I will tell you, since you believe her such a young girl." He stared Jane straight in the eye. "She has my son. She is my wife."

Jane couldn't accept what he said. "She told me her child's father was dead. Killed by bandits."

"Only a wish of hers. She ran away from me."

"With what I see, I believe I know why. This no place for her."

"And I allowed her to leave. That's what she wanted." He gritted his teeth in anger. "But she had no right to take my son from me."

"She's the child's mother. You can't separate them."

"A girl I would allow. But not a boy. He will be like me."

His firm tone sealed the finality of his words. Jane couldn't afford to anger him further. Since Adela was safe in Langtry surrounded by armed men, a tactic of indifference might prove useful. "Then let me go. And then you can find her."

It took a moment before his wide grin returned. "You are very smart. No, I will not do that. You will find rangers and they will come to find me. Maybe I leave you for *mi amigos*? Or I take you to Mexico and trade you for bullets and food?" He walked to the center of the camp. "While I am deciding which of these two for you, I will," he paused as if to think of a word, "what do you Americans call . . . have sport?"

Confused as to his meaning, she feared he might have meant her. "At least have the decency to cover my front."

As if considering an idea of little merit, he shook his head. "No." He faced the Indians. "*Traigan los gringos aqui, ahora.*" Loud chants and cheers ensued. Two Indians ran into the camp dragging Cole by a rope bound to his hands. Another pair dragged Serge Mouton in the same manner. Both men had bruises and cuts about their faces.

Blood trickled from Cole's mouth. For a moment his eyes met hers. She swallowed hard in an attempt to convey her remorse for her part in putting them in this calamity. His head sank to the dirt and so did her heart. She as much as sentenced him here.

Another rustle from behind froze her nerves. It sounded as if something crept through the bushes, like a snake.

"Don't make a sound," was whispered.

The voice sounded familiar. She kept her

eyes forward as Gura enjoyed taunting both men on the ground to the delight of the Indians. "Who's there?"

"Miles Perry. Don't give away my position. I found the horse and mule and followed the tracks here."

"What do you plan to do?"

"Nothing. Not until they're distracted. There's too many of them."

The major was right, although Jane hated to agree. Whatever was to happen would have to go on before an advantage could be gained. Cole and Mouton were yanked to their feet. Gura inspected them as if a prospective buyer of horses. Mouton looked at him with a pleading face.

"Monsieur, you must let me go. We are partners together, yes? We work together, for the glory of us both and our people."

Gura shook his head. "No, senor. We are no longer partners. You promised the rifles. My men and I went to Del Rio as you said, but nothing with your name was there."

"I swear to you I put them on the train in San Antonio. They are in a trunk with my name under a false bottom."

"And I swear to you!" Gura shouted. "They are not there. The rifles, the ones you promised, are not in my hands. I cannot chase them across Texas. It was you who were to put them in my hands. And you did not." With a slight shake of his head, he snickered. "You are no longer *mi amigo*, senor." He went to Cole. "And you are the gunman they bring. They told me you killed three of their brothers. They wanted to kill you, but I told them not to let you die so easily." He turned to the Indians. "*Muchachos, quieren ver una pelea?*"

"Do you know what he is saying?" Perry asked Jane. A loud cheer erupted from the mass of Indians.

"He's asking them if they want the men to fight."

Gura motioned to one of his men, and they cut the ropes from the captives. Then each man was bound to the other by their right hands. Gura picked up Cole's gunbelt from the ground next to Mouton's rifle and pouch. He drew the bowie knife and threw it in the fire, sticking the blade into glowing coals. "*Para que veamos quien es el hombre.*"

Jane cringed listening to the rebel leader. She blinked away the tears, forced to watch the two men battle like gladiators in a contest to see who could kill the other.

"What did he say?" Perry asked.

"He said, 'Then we will know who is the man.'" Once her eyes cleared, she looked into Cole's. He gave her a last look.

Cole faced his opponent. His aching ribs from numerous kicks made it hard to breathe. Mouton appeared to have received the same treatment. As shouts from the Comanches rose, Mouton leaner closer to Cole.

"Let us refuse to fight. If they mean to kill us, let us die with honor."

At first, Cole didn't think much of the idea, but as he gave it more mind, he knew there was no reprieve for the winner. Killing a man for a few more minutes of life wouldn't serve much purpose. As he thought more about his fate, he relaxed his right arm. Gura fired a small pistol. Mouton dove for the knife.

Surprised, Cole leaned back keeping Mouton inches away from the weapon. The Belgian screamed, punching Cole to the ground, which felled both of them. Cole squirmed to get the man off him. Fingers gouged his eyes. He rammed his palm under Mouton's chin. He strained to push the chin, and once the pressure on his eyes eased only slightly, he rolled to the left. Mouton hit the dirt facefirst. Cole slammed his left fist into Mouton's jaw, but a backhand to his own had the two roll nearer to the fire.

Mouton crawled, stretching his left arm, his fingers nudging the knife handle. Cole pulled back with his right arm and clutched his left hand on Mouton's right wrist. He tugged with such force, it brought the Belgian to his feet. With his enemy about to leap upon him, Cole drove both boot heels in Mouton's gut and thrust the man's body farther from the fire, allowing Cole a chance to gain the knife.

His right arm stretched across his chest, he bent forward toward the flame. As he did, the arm was wrenched over his left shoulder. With the bend of his own elbow cupped over his throat and Mouton's boot pressed into his back, he was being choked with his own arm. With his muscles stressed, he couldn't muster the strength to pull back. The lack of air dizzied his brain. The flames blurred into a single amber glow. In precious seconds, he'd fall in a daze and be easy prey. He pushed his arm over his chin, nose, eyes and finally over his head, which yanked him atop the Belgian.

Cole punched him twice. Filled with fury, he knew a jab to the throat would end the battle, but a knee to his groin stunned him. He lost his balance and fell to the side. The binding rope began to fray. Mouton bit at the knot, providing slack for his hand to pull free. He scrambled for the knife, but was stopped by Cole's grip on his boot.

The Belgian reached a flamed stick and swung it into Cole's face. Embers burned his eyes. Wiping them for an instant, he knew Mouton had the knife. Cole got to his feet. His smeared vision allowed only the radiance of the flame. He raised his arms and stepped back. The flame swooped from side to side in front of him. He saw the glint of a knife blade. Steel sliced into his arm.

In retreat, he blinked to clear his focus. The rush of the passing flame drew his attention. The knife's sharp point cut his thumb. He stepped farther back, ignoring the torch to try and see the knife. Fire singed his ear and hair. He batted it away, widening his eyes to spot Mouton lunging at him with the knife.

He wrapped his palms around Mouton's hand as he fell backward from the attacker's charge. The impact stabbed the point into Cole's gut. He wailed, but maintained his grasp. If he let it slip, the full length of the blade would be plunged into him. The Comanches cheered, pounding the dirt, expecting Cole to die. Mouton let out a frenzied scream, pushing at the knife, but Cole pulled the point from his flesh. His arms aching, he inched the blade over his gut to his chest.

Mouton lifted his knees. On his toes he drove his prone weight down on the knife. Trembling, Cole sensed his grip begin to slip from the handle. With the point under his jaw he twisted it up with all his might. The tip touched Mouton's throat. Sweat eroding his grasp, Cole kicked the Belgian's foot, sending Mouton down. Cole shoved the blade through the Belgian's throat and was showered with blood. With the slumped body on top of him, he exhaled in relief.

Sucking air into his lungs, he rolled out from under the corpse. He got to a knee and took a wobbled step, but his head spun from fatigue. He crashed to both knees and fell to the ground. From the corner of his eye, a Comanche with a knife came from the mass. The Indian grabbed Cole's hair and held the blade's edge ready to slice into the scalp. With muscles drained of energy, Cole couldn't lift his arms to fight anymore.

Gunshots ripped the air. The Comanche's chest became bloodied. Two more shots were fired. Cole looked up to see Miles Perry running into the camp at him.

"Get up."

Cole pushed himself to his knees. After a single breath, he climbed to his feet and Perry continued to fire. The Indians scattered into the brush except the three that writhed on the ground. The confusion would last only seconds. Standing, Cole grabbed his gunbelt and tossed Perry the Mouton rifle. The two kept firing into the brush. Jane stood freed from the tree and waved them to escape. The three of them dashed into the dark, all the while looking over their shoulders.

"The horses are just beyond this rise," said Perry.

Winded, Cole pushed his legs forward with the hope he wouldn't stumble. If he fell, he wasn't sure he could rise again. The sting from his wounds robbed his concentration. His right thumb felt numb so he passed the Colt to his left hand so he could fire.

"They're here," yelled Perry.

The major handed Cole the palomino's reins. Instinct had him mount. His hat was still on the horn, so he slammed it on his head. He followed Perry's voice.

"This way."

Chapter Fifteen

"Do you think they're behind us?" Jane asked.

Cole reined the palomino around, circling the slower mule. "I ain't going back to look. Comanches are the best trackers there is. They don't need my help." He slapped the horse's rump. "Just keep riding."

The moon dipped behind the high cliffs. Cole followed Major Perry into the shadow cast by the rocks. The difference in the light would last only minutes, but it gave them time to find a place to hide or ambush whoever might chase them.

An hour ride had sweat dripping into Cole's wounds. He squeezed the reins tighter, taking his pain out on the leather. Spells of dizziness made him blink several times to keep his mind on following the major's horse. As he blinked, a spot of light appeared. Sure he was seeing things, he faced another direction but the spots weren't there. Twisting around, he again focused on the light. It was real. "Campfire."

Perry kept riding. "We don't know who's there. We can't risk it."

"Hell, ain't no Comanche gonna burn fires looking for us. It's got to be white men. Cowboys on a trail."

"And if it's not?" asked Perry as he reined in.

Cole pulled alongside and soon Jane had the mule next to him. "These horses won't make it back to Langtry at a gallop. If it is drovers, we'll need all the guns we can round up. I'd think they'd want to know if Comanches were riding in the night. We need to take the chance." Cole opened the chamber gate on the Colt. "How many you got left?"

Perry snapped up the chamber on the Schofield. "Two. I couldn't see to reload."

"Same here. Bullets are too rare to drop." In the dim shimmer of the distant light, both men expelled empty shells and loaded all cylinders. Cole peeked down at the seven cartridges left in his belt. If he did get into another gunfight, he'd better hope whoever it might be was shooting the same caliber as he. "Okay, let's go in slow and see who's in there."

The three riders ambled their horses nearer the light. Perry steered to the far side so as to enter from the opposite end. Within feet on the camp, Cole dismounted and motioned for Jane to do the same. He winced while crouching into the brush.

"Are you all right?"

"I'm okay. Just stay behind me. If there's shooting—."

"I know," she said, buttoning her shirt. "Keep my head down. I'm an expert by now."

Cole crept farther, the Colt in his left hand and hammer back. As they cleared the outer thicket of thorns, he saw an old wagon with a canvas cover. It was a shock and a welcome sight. "I'll be damned."

"I can't believe it," remarked Jane. She rose behind him and ran into the camp. "Lord Apperson! Mr. Jeffers!" she called. The two startled men came from around the wagon. Jane embraced both men as if they were long lost family. Adela too came around the side and she hugged Jane as well.

"How wonderful, my dear!" Apperson exclaimed. "I was unsure if we'd find you."

Cole came to the fire, kicking dirt into the flame. "Can't have this making it known where we are."

"Wait," Jane shouted, stopping his final kick, allowing a small flame to lick the wood. "Your shirt! Look at you!"

Cole peeked at his front. His green shirt was blackened by the moisture. The waist of his pants were stained red. "We can't keep the fire burning."

"You're bleeding too badly. Leave the fire; I'll need it to see."

Cole glanced at Perry, who led Sackhead Bob back into the light. "Look what I found," said Perry as he holstered his pistol.

"I was just heading for cover," Bob said.

"Then why were you still running away when I caught you?" The major shook his head. It showed he too knew the need to keep moving. No matter the pain, Cole wanted to ride.

"It can wait. If they find us, they'll be a lot more bleeding."

"You'll bleed to death," she said defiantly. "Take off that shirt. We'll take only enough time to save your life." Jane turned and jabbered Mex to Adela, who went to the mule and pulled a single hair from its tail and gave it to Jane. Cole opened his shirt as the woman doctor retrieved a small bag from the wagon.

"Did you locate Mouton and that Burroughs chap?" asked Apperson.

"We found him, all right," answered Perry disgusted. "We found your Belgian soldier was a turncoat."

"I won't believe that."

"It's true," Jane said as she returned to the light of the fire. "I saw him myself. He was aiding Mexican rebels. Supplying them with rifles."

"That's what got him killed. That trunk left in Langtry must have been what they were looking for."

"Good heavens." Apperson turned from Perry to look at Jeffers. "I think we have it." Jeffers nodded.

Cole looked again at Perry. "I think I'll have a look," said Perry. Cole started forward only to be pushed back in front of the fire.

"Get back there. The major can find them,"

said Jane like a mother to her son. She knelt to get her eyes level with the wound. "Open your shirt." Cole complied slowly, biting his lip while peeling the cloth from the gash in his flesh.

"There are six rifles in the false bottom, just as he said," Perry said as he came from the back of the wagon. "Poor bastard was telling the truth."

"Not so poor that I regret his loss," Jane remarked, then peered up at Cole. "Especially considering what it would mean to you."

"We can use them rifles," said Cole.

"And what of Burroughs?"

"He's dead too," Perry said.

At the news, Cole stared openmouthed at the major. He had taken a liking to the Texas Ranger captain.

Perry shook his head. "The more I think about it, the wound in his chest must have been made by this." He lifted the rifle.

"It was a horrible sight," said Jane. "I fell over his body when I ran from the Indians. It was awful. Something I don't want to be reminded of." She removed a needle, a small bottle, and a ball of cotton. Threading the mule hair through the needle, she tore a piece from the ball. Removing the bottle cap she soaked the cotton with wood alcohol and swabbed the blood from his wound.

Cole blew from the tonic's burn and flinched when she extended the needle toward his stomach.

"Don't be a child," said Jane, and she poked

the needle through his flesh. The prick made him grit his teeth. "You were almost killed, and now a needle scares you."

"Killed?" The mention surprised Apperson.

Perry walked to the center of camp. "It's true. Cole here was put in a death match against Mouton." He faced Cole. "There for a while, I thought we'd lost you."

Cole winced as Jane pulled the mule hair through his skin. "You could have shot that pistol a lot earlier. Saved me a lot of pain."

"I was busy untying Dr. Reeves. By the time I was done, you were on your back with that knife stuck in you."

"How extraordinary! Indeed, you must be all that is said about you, Mr. Cole."

Cole took no pride in Apperson's words. "Fighting for my life, I did what I had to. I ain't bragging about it." Cole faced Perry. "Just the same, Miles. Thanks for saving my scalp."

A small grin broke the major's face. "Now you owe me."

"You were lucky," said Jane as she stared at his wound. "It doesn't seem any major vessels or organs were ruptured. Another inch and I'm afraid you'd have been beyond any doctor's care." She bit through the end of the hair, pulled the slack and knotted it off.

"That was on my mind at the time," said Cole sarcastically. A sharp sting shot through his spine. "What are you doing?"

"I'm closing the suture. You'll need more care. At least you'll be able to travel."

"Traveling is what we all need be doing." Cole

buttoned the shirt. "Let's put out the fire and get out of here before the Comanches find us."

"Comanches are on your trail?" Bob squealed. He looked to Apperson. "When I said I would you bring you out here, I never said nothing about fighting. Pay me my money. I'm riding back to town."

"I wouldn't advise going to Langtry," warned Perry. "If they are searching for us, it would be the first place I'd expect them to look. The terrain is all rocks, hard to travel over with a wagon. They would pick us off on the run."

Bob went to Apperson, stuck his hand out and snatched the greenbacks. "I don't care what you say. You folks are goners if you stay out here." Bob climbed on his horse and galloped into the night.

"Little question why the man is known as Sackhead," said Perry. "My bet is he'll never make it back. But it could play to our advantage."

"How's that?"

"They'll go after him, allowing us to escape to the north."

"That's terrible," said Jane. "We can't let him go alone."

"It was his choice, Doctor. I tried to warn him."

"But you believe he'll be killed. We must go after him."

"Then we'll be killed," said Cole. "Perry is right. If we go and chase him, then we'll be an easier target than he is."

Jane put her hands on her hips. "Then you'll sacrifice him."

"If it's between him or us, there ain't no choice about it."

"Besides, Doctor," added Perry. "I would think you would want to think over another consideration." She looked at him confused. Perry's eye shifted upon Adela. Jane's firm stance seemed to shrink away.

Now Cole stood confused. "What are you two talking about?"

Slowly Perry faced him. "The Mexican girl is Gura's wife."

All eyes locked on Adela, and although she didn't speak, she hung her head with her hand to her face and ran to the back of the wagon.

"Oh, dear," said Apperson with a blank stare.

"It was him that put that baby in her belly? That's just great," Cole bellowed. "All this time, we thought they were after us. They're after her."

"And the first place they'll look, Doctor, is that tent town where we left. If we were to go back, we'd run right into them."

The logic of Perry's statement showed on Jane's face. Her resolve to continue after the foolish Bob slackened. "I better go see about her." She went to the rear of the wagon, but was stopped when Perry produced the cloth from her torn bodice. "Is this yours? I found it on Burroughs's body."

"Yes," she answered, snatching it from his hand.

"The best thing for us to do is head north, pronto. Strike this camp and let's move out." Cole dragged his foot and smothered the fire with dirt.

Chapter Sixteen

Nothing rattled Cole more than the thought that something unseen was watching him from behind. The creaking wagon didn't help his nerves either. With the Colt drawn, he kept a wary eye out for any movement as the eastern sky gradually turned from black to blue. The morning chill was made worse by a stout breeze from the west. More than once he had nearly wasted a round on swaying junipers. The advance of dawn eased the problem of sight, just as it would for whoever might be looking their way.

He rode around the wagon once more as he had several times during the night. As he neared the seat box, he reined in. "You need to put more step in that team. It'll be light soon."

Jeffers nodded in response and snapped the

reins. From out of the dark, Major Perry rode at a gallop from the north.

"I don't see anything to oppose our path. Neither man nor land. We can follow this valley right in the grassland and into Fort Concho."

"It'll take two days maybe more to get that far at this pace."

"Well," said Perry, "I could ride ahead and bring soldiers back with me."

"By the time you come back, we would have been there. I'd as soon not be without your gun for that long."

Perry inhaled a long breath to show he felt his pride had been smudged. "I could be back here no later than noon tomorrow. You could hold your position here."

"We ain't making no stand out here; I'd have to . . . fire . . . every . . ." Cole's attention on the discussion waned with the distant but increasing sound of a horse's hooves pounding the ground. He scanned each direction as did Perry. The noise seemed strongest from the pitch-black of the west. The squeak from the wagon wheels began to slow, because Apperson and Jeffers too were interested in who was riding their way.

"Keep that wagon moving." Cole held the palomino steady as he raised the Colt and prepared to take aim on the rider as soon as he could make out whoever it was. Perry cocked the hammer of his revolver. Gradually, the rider emerged wearing chaps and a stetson and he yelled a loud cry.

"Help me! They're right behind—" A gunshot

sent a ripple through the air. The horseman toppled to the ground, and a loud wail came from out of the dark.

"It sounds like that idiot Bob," said Perry.

"I think you're right." The wagon wheels stopped. Cole looked back to the east and saw Jane climb out from the rear. "Get back in that wagon!"

"I heard a shot. Is someone hurt?"

"I said get your tail back in that wagon!"

"Here they come."

Cole twisted upon Perry's words. Four hatless riders came from the west at a gallop. "That damn fool led them right back to us." He fired, the muzzle flash blinding him for an instant. He didn't know if he hit his target, so he spurred the palomino as Perry shot and turned his mount.

"Slap leather on them ponies!" Cole shouted. "Get that wagon moving." He peered over his shoulder. His jarred view in the dark couldn't discern whether the attackers had fled or were seeking cover. In either case, he didn't like being a target, so he rode to catch up with the wagon. Jane clung to the rear of the canvas, her feet dangling near the dirt. With the team charging over the rocky ground, she sagged further with every jolt.

Cole steered his mount along to her side. He stretched his right arm and grabbed her around the waist, reining the palomino just clear of the wheels. As he clutched her to his hip, the team ran where two slopes converged. As the horse leapt over the gully, the front left wheel crashed into the hill, spinning it off the spindle.

Among screams and whinnies, the wagon tipped over. The canvas cover snapped its mooring and flew in the wind. Perry kicked his horse to catch the driverless team. Once he gained a hold on the harness, the wagon slid to a stop.

Cole reined the palomino to a stop and set Jane on the ground. She ran between the bows and rifled through the debris. A baby's cry was a welcome sound. Out of the dark shadows cast by the wagon, Jane knelt next to something that moved on its own. An instant later, Adela rose out of the shadows.

"She's says she's all right."

With Jane's relieved voice, Cole went to the overturned box. A teetering Apperson rubbed his head, his head slumped to his chest. While the east grew lighter, Cole saw the upper body of Jeffers, trapped at the waist by the weight of the wagon's broadside. Swinging his leg over the palomino, Cole hit the ground and ran to try and lift it.

Each shove against the weight produced an anguished moan from the old man. Jane, Perry and Apperson crowded around, all joining Cole in attempting to right the wagon. As Perry and Cole pushed, slowly raising the wagon, Apperson and the two women pulled Jeffers from under the boards.

"Oh, dear God," Jane uttered in shock. Cole went by her side as she tore through Jeffers's blood-soaked shirt. "His ribs are broken and have punctured the skin." She looked again at the bleeding wound. After another moment, she glanced at Cole and shook her head twice.

"They're coming again!" Perry yelled.

Cole stood to shield those around Jeffers. "Take cover!"

"We can't move him!" Jane shouted.

"Then leave him or you'll be tending your own bullet holes." Cole and Perry fired at two advancing Comanches. One fell limp into the brush while the other dove.

"They'll try for position," said Perry. He went around to the upturned floor of the wagon while Cole took a knee. Apperson, Jane and Adela crouched low to the ground.

Cole cocked the Colt's hammer and waited for something to move. The plain before him was still. Even the air became calm. "What do you think?"

"I think they're prepared to wait us out until their reinforcements get here. Surely, they heard the shots," Perry answered.

"How many do you count?"

"Four at the start. But it was dark. I'd guess no more than that even with the loss of one."

The darkness of the west faded as the yellow light of the dawn crept over the horizon. Brown, gray and green emerged on the land. Awkward figures took shape as tangled yuccas. A mild beat broke the silence. Just over the crest of the plain, a rider kicked his pony in retreat from the scene.

"There's goes one," Perry said as he raised the rifle to his shoulder. "Let's give this a try." A moment passed before the blast of the shot echoed. The rider was still mounted. He took another shot and the result remained the same.

"Quit wasting bullets. That's what they want," Cole ordered. "We ain't waiting around for their friends. Unhook them draft horses and ride out."

"I'm not leaving Jeffers," Apperson staunchly announced.

"Suit yourself," said Cole as he stepped over Jeffers.

A crackling scream came from the brush. An agonized cry of continual pain. After few seconds, Cole knew who it was and the purpose of the sound.

"What is it?" Jane turned to him, her eyes wide and mouth open. Cole paused only a moment and continued to the horses.

"We got to move."

She rose and grabbed his arm. "Tell me. What are they doing? Who's out there?"

"It's Sackhead Bob. It's a trick to keep us here." Although hesitant to tell her the reason, he thought the truth might convince her of the need to leave. Amid more shrills, he paused while unhitching the horses then looked her in the eye. "They're skinning him."

She trembled, her jaw quivered. "Oh, dear God," she said, covering her mouth. "What . . . what are we going to do? We have to help him." She turned about as if to head to the brush, but he grabbed her arm and twisted her around.

"We ain't going out there."

"But they're killing him."

"He's dead already. Don't you see, they want to draw us out there so they can kill us, too. There ain't nothing we can do for him now." His words made her stare as if in a trance. He shook her arm. "Get that girl and old man. We're riding out of here."

After several moments, she nodded twice and went to where Adela and Apperson knelt over Jeffers.

"We must leave," she said. "Before we're all killed." She took Adela's arm and the Mexican girl slowly rose, wrapping her baby tighter in her arms. Jane then placed her hand on the English Lord's shoulder. "We must go."

"I'm not leaving without him. I'm staying, do you hear me?"

Amid gurgled breath, Jeffers struggled to speak. "Please, sir, leave me."

"Kenneth, don't be silly. You don't know what you're saying. We British never leave behind our wounded."

Jeffers slowly put his palm on his Apperson's cheek. "Nigel, this once, do what I tell you. I'll be fine. Take care of yourself." Jeffers' jaw fell agape. The hand slowly slipped from the cheek and rapidly slumped to the ground.

"It's time. There's nothing we can do for him now."

With his eyes squinted shut, Apperson embraced his friend for the last time, then released the body to lay in the dirt. He got to his feet just as the screams from the brush ceased.

"Sounds like Bob played out. Let's go!" Cole

shouted. He lifted Adela onto one of the horses. The trailing Apperson, his aimless stumbling walk making him an easier target, had to be led by Jane's hand. Cole cupped his palms as a stirrup. Jane guided the old man's foot into them, and he was boosted atop the mount. Finally, Cole took hold of Jane's hips and put her on a horse.

Shots wildly fired boomed from the bushes.

Perry rode to the front, cradling the rifle in his arms. "I don't think they want us to leave."

Cole mounted the palomino and he led the four other riders. "Let's head for those hills." More shots echoed. Peeking over his shoulder, he spotted two men on ponies coming from the far brush. He pointed in the direction and yelled at Perry, "They're coming after us!"

The major peeled back. Cole slapped the rumps of the three bareback mounts to keep them running. Adela held her child tightly while barely managing a grip of the horse's mane. Jane and Apperson did the same, but Cole then feared a full gallop might throw the lot of them.

As they reached high grass, he reined in and looked back at Perry. The major aimed the rifle at the two pursuers, but they stopped their chase and held their ponies. Cole figured they were near a half mile away. As he was about to call for Perry to fall back, a booming eruption cracked the morning air. One of the riders dropped from the pony like a grain sack tumbling over. The other pony reared and nearly threw its rider, but once all four hooves settled, the rider turned the animal to scamper off. Perry pumped the action and fired once more, and both horse and rider fell. Only the pony rose to continue its gallop.

Major Perry rode back with a gleaming smile. "Say what you want about that bastard Mouton. This weapon is everything he claimed it to be."

"It sure is loud enough, I'll give it that. That echo will carry for miles. It won't be long before the rest of them find us." Both men turned their mounts and caught the others, whose horses were at an amble.

"What now?" asked Jane.

"Now we find a place we can defend. I don't think we'll make it one night in open country. If we don't spot any more of them for a few days, then we might try to make a run for it."

"A few days?" she remarked. "All of our water is back at that wagon. All our supplies, our food. What will we drink or eat?"

"You want to go back for it? You think you can tote that barrel on your lap? We'll have to make do with what we got. I've got a full canteen and so does the major. We'll ration the water and we'll live off what we find to eat."

"And what if we find nothing?"

"Lady," Cole said through gritted teeth, "we're heading this way. If you don't want to be left behind, then you'll keep your animal in line with ours."

He stared her straight in the eye. Moments went by without a word from anyone. Jane's pursed lips and flushed cheeks showed the fire burning inside her. He knew any woman, especially a redhead, didn't take to being growled at, but neither did he take to being nagged by a woman so soon after being shot at by hostiles.

Just as she opened her mouth seemingly to breathe fire, Apperson pointed ahead and all eyes shifted in the direction. "Good heavens, look there." A black swirl funneled out from a distant butte. "Smoke. Someone is burning a fire. That's a sign of good fortune, that. We should go there. Surely, we could seek help from whomever is there."

"I didn't like the idea last time," muttered Perry.

"Yeah, and you were wrong," Cole replied. He gazed upon the scattering plume, and although there wasn't a doubt it was really there, the pattern wasn't something he'd seen before. There was little breeze blowing, but the top of the plume seemed to travel level with the ground. However, that wasn't the most peculiar. "If I had to guess, the smoke is going down instead of up."

"You're right," Jane said. "The spiral is descending. And it's not smoke." She faced Cole. "Those are bats."

Chapter Seventeen

The twisting spiral of bats lasted long enough for the party to follow. With the Colt drawn, Cole dismounted and crept to the rim of a horseshoe gulch. Jane and the others remained in the outer brush as he lay prone and inched his way to peek over the edge. Rocks and boulders of various size littered the sandy floor, which stretched into the plain to the end of his view. As he craned his neck further, he saw the small opening of a cave below him that either served as the source or the mouth of an ancient waterflow.

Whether due to the absence of any sign of life or his own fatigue draining his senses, several minutes went by before he was confident enough to stand. Soon, he was joined by the others. Jane and Apperson gawked with awe and curiosity. They proceeded down the rocky slope step by shaky step. Cole glanced at Perry. The two men agreed without words they were too tired from the night's events to argue for caution.

They followed the other three, Cole supporting Adela's arm as they descended to the bottom of the gulch. Jane led with the vigor of a commanding officer, charging up jagged stones to climb into the cave's mouth. When Cole came to stand next to her, she and Apperson stared blankly into the opaque interior.

"What an extraordinary stroke of luck," said the Englishman.

"How you mean?"

"A respite, Mr. Cole. I for one can use one. How about you, Jane?"

"Yes. Without question." She stepped over a small ridge and into the opening. When she took two more steps, a hissed rattle broke the silence.

"Don't move," Cole ordered. The sound was unmistakable. He leaned over her shoulder and peered at the shadowy crevices, but couldn't lay eyes on the snake.

"Can I move now?" she asked in a quivering voice.

"Not until I know where it is," he whispered. "It could be right under you. They'll strike at sudden movement."

Perry, having led the horses down the slope, ascended to the cave. "What's wrong?"

Cole raised his hand to be still.

Jane trembled. The rattle became more rapid.

"Clay, please do something. My hands are shaking. I can't keep them still."

He eased a knee to the ground and peered about the holes and cracks and listened. The sound was greater under the curved lip of the ridge beneath his own chest. He extended his bare hand and touched Jane's leg. "Step out."

Once she did, the rattle remained consistent. The snake had locked onto a new target. Cole spread his thumb from his fingers and opened his left palm. He propped his right fist over the palm so give the snake something else to concentrate on and reached closer to the ridge. The rattle increased, yet Cole still continued. A diamondback's head launched from the dark. Cole clamped his palm just under its drooped jaw. Once secure in his grip of the viper, fangs in clear display, Cole looked up at Jane. "You said you were hungry?"

She exhaled in a huff. "That's not funny."

"I wasn't joking." He stood and held the snake at arm's length. "I'd say there's about five or six feet of meat there. It's good eating."

"Good show, old boy. I thought he had you there for a moment."

"You weren't the only one," replied Cole as he drew his knife.

"How are you going to cook it?"

The answer seemed simple, but he quickly remembered that he had lit his last match to illuminate the sculpture. "Oh, I guess we'll have to eat it raw." he said while casually slicing off the snake's head. Jane's cringed lips had him notice where the head had fallen. "Careful of that. The varmint can still bite you."

With closed eyes, she inhaled and exhaled a deep breath, all the while shaking her head. She stepped farther into the cave, followed by Apperson, who put his hand to his paunch.

"A bit of a weak stomach, I'm afraid."

As Adela went by, she shielded her son away from the dangling serpent. Finally, Major Perry trudged up the steep slope leading the horses. He peered at the snake, then looked Cole in the eye. "Not on your life." He too went into the cave.

"It ain't that bad, honest." Soon Cole found himself alone just outside of the opening. "Suit yourselves. When your bellies start aching, don't say I didn't offer you none."

The glare off the rocks faded. Cole glanced up to see a line of clouds covering the sun. "That figures," he muttered to himself. "We find shade just as it gets cloudy." As he entered the cave, his skin was soothed by cool air. Careful of his step, he sat next to Jane who held her head in her hands. Apperson settled prone on the ground and a glance at Adela showed her tending to her baby's hunger. Perry finished securing the horses to stand on the sparse level ground and he joined Cole and Jane.

"How long should we wait?" asked Perry as he opened his collar.

"As long as we can, maybe until nightfall. If we haven't spotted any of them, we may give thought to sneaking away."

"Wait an entire day? An hour maybe, two at the most, but we can't stay here."

Cole stabbed the knife point into the snake's belly. "Don't seem like a bad idea to me."

"Of course not. Why does that not surprise me?"

The officer's remark drew Cole's attention. "How you mean that?"

"Let's just say, your past suggests reluctance to act."

Jane raised her head with Perry's bitter words.

"What are you getting at, Major?" Cole asked, resuming his focus on the snake. He ran the blade down, splitting the skin open in the middle.

"I'm saying that after a short rest we should leave here and try to make it to Fort Concho."

"And I say that's a damn fool idea."

"Would you rather sit still and be slaughtered?"

"I'd think better of my chances in a place where my back ain't open for an arrow."

"This cave?" Perry pointed into the dark. "We don't even know where it leads. For all we know, there's another entrance, one they might know. Then we would be trapped."

"You think trying to outrun Comanches in open country is a gravy lick? They'd run us down in no time." Cole paused, spite filling his thoughts. "Oh, I forgot. You think a lot of the idea of charging against a force where you're outnumbered ten to one."

Perry furrowed his brow. "At least I wouldn't

be in the camp of the enemy." Cole dropped the snake and stood, knife in hand. Perry rose as well as if to meet the challenge.

"Stop it, both of you," Jane ordered. "I thought you had settled your differences. We won't last long if you two choose to fight each other. Just what is it between you that drives you to want to kill each other?"

The woman's sobering words had Cole feel the knife handle in his palm. He looked away from the major, realizing the truth of what she said. After a moment, he sat on the rock again and picked up the snake carcass, but Perry still stood.

"I guess you're right," he admitted. "Might do some good to get it off our chests. You want to tell her or should I?"

Drawing a long breath, Perry pushed his hat back and faced Jane. "Five years ago, almost to the day, I was with the Seventh Calvary as part of an expeditionary force to find Sioux and Cheyenne hostiles who refused to return to the reservation. We were given orders to pursue a large band which had gathered in Montana near a river the Crow scouts called the Greasy Grass."

"That ain't all they said," Cole blurted, then looked to Jane. "I was with them scouts and I talked to them. They told me they saw the biggest group of tribes ever seen. Maybe as many as three thousand warriors. But Custer didn't give that any mind. He was the Boy General, the Great Yellow Hair, Son of the Morning Star. He was drunk on his own glory. He didn't think he could lose."

"I thought I was telling this," said Perry. Cole held out his palms in surrender. After a moment, Perry continued. "It is true our scouts had found a large force of the enemy. Just as was predicted by our knowledge of the Sioux. They had joined together to hunt buffalo. General Terry wanted to surround them from the east, west, and south. But General Crook had previously failed to establish a southern perimeter. We knew this, and we couldn't allow the Sioux to escape. That's when we were ordered to find them." He looked at Cole. "But then we were betrayed."

Cole felt Jane's eyes shift to him while he returned Perry's glare. "You know that ain't the way it was."

"Isn't it? Are you denying your part?"

"I ain't denying nothing." He faced Jane. "I was given secret orders."

"He swears they were from President Grant."

"They were," Cole retorted. "Grant and Custer snarled at each other like a hound and bobcat. Grant knew when given the chance, Custer would jump his leash and Grant didn't want no more bloodshed." Cole looked to Perry. "They weren't supposed to attack. The orders were to join Terry and wait."

"We had been spotted," Perry shot back. "We had no choice."

"And three hundred troopers were wiped out."

"They wouldn't have had we not been betrayed." The two men sternly faced each other. Jane's calm voice broke the standoff.

"So, is it true?"

"No," said Cole. He removed his hat to rub his forehead. "President Grant knew I was scouting with the Seventh. I got a message from him to get to Sitting Bull and try to talk sense in him. But I couldn't let it be known what I was doing. I never got the chance. I was captured and tied to a tree with a rock stuck in my mouth so as to shut me up. I still thought once the army came, the Lakota would change their mind, to see they were surrounded. But, instead of giving them time to think about it, Custer came charging without support from Terry."

"And when we did, we would have subdued them, had blundering officers not been cowards." Perry swallowed hard. "I wanted to be at his side, but he ordered me to join Major Marcus Reno. We crossed the Little Big Horn river and made our assault on the camp. I admit, we did encounter heavy resistance, but I'm convinced, if we pressed on, we would have distracted the Sioux enough to give Custer's charge a chance. But Reno ordered retreat. We fell back, soldiers scrambling backward rather than running forward, shot like a covey of birds trying to take flight. We took cover in the hills and were surprised to find Captain Benteen at our flank, rather than at Custer's. While we waited for another wave of attackers, I could hear the shots from over the next valley."

"It was Custer," said Cole. "That's what I was looking at. It was only minutes after he came charging down that he was flushed back up that hill, covered with Lakota and Cheyenne firing Henry repeaters. Once I didn't hear any more shots and saw the bucks returning with army hats and shirts, I knew Custer was dead."

After a long silence, Jane put her palm on Cole's hand. "What a terrible memory for both of you. Maybe it's time to put it behind."

"Never," Perry said. "Not until I bring him before a military court."

"Well, that's one thing I agree with you on, Miles. I want to be done with it as much as you. Still, I believe nobody knows what all really happened on that day. And I don't think all the truth ever will be known."

Perry straightened his hat. "Someone should act as a sentry if we intend to stay here." He picked up the Mouton rifle and walked to the outside. Cole resumed gutting the snake.

"I had no idea you carried such a burden," said Jane. "With what you told me about your father's death, it seems you've only known tragedy in your life."

At first, he was inclined to agree, however, as he reflected on the events of his life, he felt the knotted red bandanna around his neck. "It hasn't all been so bad."

"Why do you say that?"

"In New Mexico, near a town called Nobility, is a farm with a widow woman and her son and daughter. They needed some help. Someone burnt down their barn. I didn't have nothing at the time due to a thief having ambushed me for my gun and clothes." He paused a moment as more memories came to mind. "Me and the boy took to each other right off. It was like he was mine, like my boy." A grin broke his face.

"We cut down trees up in the hills to build the barn with and I taught him how to shoot an old cap-and-ball musket, and it was like it was real, like I was his pa."

"And what about the mother and the girl?"

"Well, the little girl, she didn't take to me at first. She acted kinda scared. After a while though, I think she warmed up to me, and I have to say it took me a while. I don't know about little girls too good." He waited to answer the rest of the question, occupying his attention on carving the muscle from the snake. He offered a blade full of meat to her at which she sneered. "Go on. I know you're hungry. You ate armadillo."

Reluctantly, she took it with her fingertips from the blade, huffed out a quick breath for courage and slowly placed it on her tongue. After the initial bite, she raised her eyebrows and chewed and swallowed it naturally. "Not bad. Not bad at all."

"Told you," he said, while cutting himself a piece and popped it in his mouth.

"You didn't finish."

"Huh?"

"You didn't finish telling me about the mother of the children."

Although he was normally not accustomed to telling his private thoughts, a solace came over him as he shared the personal memory. "Well, she was something special. At first, she didn't think much of me. More than once, I had a mind to light out, but every time I asked her if she needed me to, she had a look about her that I took to mean that I should stay. It's hard to put words to it to how she looked. She never said so, neither." He cut out another clump and gave it to her.

"So you two . . . became friends?"

With his mouth full, he nodded then cleared his throat. "You could say that."

"Why did you leave?"

"When trouble follows you around like a dog and when you can't shake it from you," he paused, and a small smirk came over his face, "the only thing to do is take it with you away from the folks that hadn't got nothing to do with it."

"That's very thoughtful." She raised her hand politely to decline further helpings of the meat. "Do you think you'll go back?"

Wearing the same smirk, he nodded. "I'd like to hope so, someday." His smirk faded. "But, until I can clear my name, there ain't much chance of that happening."

"Perhaps the Rhodes woman will be successful in helping you do that?"

The smirk returned. "Well, she is a stickler for what she sets her mind to. I'll give her that. Kind of like you."

"Really?" The comparison seemed to surprise her. "In what way?"

"Yeah," he answered, flinging the carcass outside, noticing the rocks again basked in sunlight. "You both speak Mex, for one. I guess that says a lot for schooling back East. I don't know many white folks that bothered to learn the lingo, much less women."

She paused a moment. "I'll take that as a compliment, I guess."

"And you're a little bigger than she is." Upon his remark, Jane began looking at herself. "Oh, I don't mean *big* bigger, like man big," he tried to explain. He waved his hand in the general area of her torso. "Just some things . . . about you . . . that you got . . . are . . . bigger."

"Oh," she said, showing she understood his reference. "We all come in different . . . forms?"

Cole nodded, relieved his slip of the tongue didn't require further explanation. "And the two of you do make a feisty pair. You ain't scared of talking back to men. Even those you ain't married to."

"I presume to take that as a compliment, as well." A smirk grew on her face. "I'll have to make it a point to visit her, since we have so much in common."

"Wouldn't be a bad idea. After you get back to your family."

Her smirk faded and her eyes darted to the ground. "I don't have much family left in Boston." Her tone showed regret. "My father and mother have passed on. I had an elder brother, but he was killed in the war. That's why I understood the effect of the loss of your father. My father wanted him to be a doctor just as he, but Stephen was an adventurer, that's why he joined the fighting."

"And so your pa wanted you to be a doctor to make up for your brother?"

"Hardly. My father never wanted anything for me but to become married and raise his grandchildren. However, I was intrigued by his work and convinced him to allow me to enter college, even with the promise that one day I would get married. But, once in school, I found another love. That of the learning about the unknown. Neither of my parents approved. A career isn't an appropriate pursuit for a daughter. But I kept on with my studies and became enamored with the work of William H. Prescott. I read his books over and over, particularly *The Conquest of Mexico*, and Cortes's own letters to Spain. I found my true calling, archeology. There was never any time for anything or anyone else."

"So you broke your promise?"

She met his eyes. "I'm not dead. Thanks in large part to you." She looked at his hand. "By the way, how are you?"

"A heap better," he answered, wiggling his thumb. "Getting the feel back in it, most of the tingle is gone." As he wiggled, he was distracted by motion on the ground. "Same with . . . my gut." The motion became more visible with each second. An instant later, he recognized the shape. It was the shadowed outline of his thumb.

He looked to Jane, who also seemed bewildered by the ever-increasing light behind them. At first a dim gray, it brightened with every breath he took. Both of their silhouettes emerged before them. The rock walls glistened. The source of the light was at their backs, so Cole palmed the butt of the Colt but didn't draw it. Whatever was behind had the drop on them and he didn't want to be shot. He cautiously twisted about.

"Oh, my God," Jane said with awe. "What day is it?"

"Ain't got no idea," he mumbled as he turned. Brilliant illumination showed them standing atop a precipice overlooking a cavernous area. A monument with four sides of masoned stone steps escalated from the floor to the top. Cole froze, moving only his eyes to view the radiant white figure at the top of the monument. It was a skull of glass the size of a house, butting against the roof of the cave, shining so intensely, he squinted from the glow.

Apperson quickly got to his feet while Adela sank to her knees and crossed herself in prayer. Jane stood motionless as did Cole. Rays of light shot out from the eye sockets. Bats flapped into the air, swirling about the cave, careening into the walls and all that stood in their way. Cole swatted them away from his head and so did Jane. Adela screamed from the swarm as Apperson continued to gaze upon the site unperturbed. Major Perry charged into the cave only to come to a quick halt next to Cole. The bats soon took refuge in the few darker shadows and the view became clear. The luminous skull lit up the interior like the sun.

"I don't believe it," said Perry. "It can't be."

"Precisely what others have said, Major," Apperson said, then he looked to Jane. "You've done it, my dear. You've done it!"

Chapter Eighteen

Jane stood entranced by the glittering mixture of red, orange and white hues on the stalactites above. Suddenly, pieces of the puzzling riddle became clear. "It all makes sense." She faced Cole. "The entwined lines on the sculpture. They were the bats in flight. The figure looking to the north at a skull. This skull!"

"Yeah, but how does the glass let in that much light?"

"It's a crystal. Made to refract the sun's light and project it. There must be a hole in the roof to allow it in. The Aztecs were artisans as well as astute astronomers. That's why the solstice; the sun's exact position in the sky is the only time when it is possible. The clouds must have blocked the light before we came in. It's just as in the letter. The sun will open the chamber."

"And so it has," Apperson said. "And so it has."

"I don't see any treasure," Perry decried.

"And we shall search for it," Apperson mused. "Just as spelunkers in search of primitive etchings." He carefully began the trek down the jagged descending steps cut into the precipice like a staircase.

The intensity of the rays weakened. "I suppose we should hurry," she said to Cole. "The light won't last very long. Only while the sun is overhead." As she followed Apperson's eager lead, the cooler air surrounded her the lower she descended.

Unable to keep her eyes off the small and large cone stalagmites jutting up from the rocks, her foot slipped from under her. She fell back and found herself in Cole's cradling embrace. His warm breath wafted on her chilled cheeks. The light cast a shadow over one side of his face. His lips were inches from hers.

"You okay?"

It took a moment to clear her thoughts. "Yes, I'm fine." She regained her balance, both on her feet and in her mind. "The footing is damp from condensation."

"I see that."

Inhaling the brisk air helped her focus on negotiating the steps. A peek behind showed Adela and Major Perry following with equal caution. Finally they arrived on the more secure bottom.

"Where to now?" asked Cole.

"I can't be sure," she replied. Although the rays were clearly visible, she could sense the minor loss of light. She went to touch the crafted stonework of the pyramid. "This is remarkable. The markings show signs of the Mayan culture. It must have taken decades to excavate the interior and construct it inside here. It could be centuries older than we think."

"I thought we didn't have much time."

Tempted to examine further, Perry's remark snatched her wistful mood away. "Of course. You're right." She peered upward, unable to take her eyes off the rays. The cylindrical beams shone farther into the depths of the cavern over rock walls that didn't extend to the top. Since there wasn't a final point at which they ended, she concluded their purpose was by design.

"They may have hidden the trinkets among the stones here," Apperson suggested.

"No," Jane replied. "They wouldn't have laid them carelessly about."

She continued to stare at the rays. They resembled beacons so she walked warily in their direction. She stubbed her foot against a rise in the floor. Upon glancing down she noticed squared slabs placed like tiles. The path took her even lower in the cave. It led into a tunnel through the rock walls, winding to the left and then to the right.

Her breath fogged when she exhaled, and her arms and chest shivered due to the dank air. She rubbed warmth into her skin while ducking a low overhang and stepping over a small fissure. The mosaic of colors in the tunnel diverted her attention and she stumbled over another fissure, falling on hands and knees just as she reached the opening. The moisture on the tile gleamed, but not from the light that was behind her but from that which emanated in front.

She raised her head slowly. A shimmering amber glow reflected off an immense round calendar of gold. The discovery stole her breath. She drank in the view of an Aztec temple cordoned by golden figurines encircling a single gold statue. It stood on a altar placed in front of the calendar.

As if commanded to rise before an ancient deity, she got to her feet. She sensed the others surrounding her, but her eyes remained fixed on the site. Her entire attention was held captive by the radiance. Finally, she inhaled. The cold air awakened her perception.

She was distracted by Apperson falling to his knees and clasping his hands in prayer. The Englishman wept. She knew they were the tears of a dream realized.

"We found it," he cried. "Hidden from the eyes of mankind for three hundred years."

"I must hand it to you, Doctor. So this is the vault where they stored their treasure."

"It's not a vault, Major Perry. It is a shrine." Compelled to inspect further, she approached the gold statue. Standing as tall as she, it was the sculpted idol of a warrior holding a sword with a snake's head serving as the blade. In the other hand it held a shield of feathers just as those projecting from its crowning headdress, which flowed into a cape angling down the back. It wore a breastplate painted in blue. A mask covered the face with blue opals mounted in the eye holes.

"Huitzilopochtli," she murmured. "The patron god of the Mexica that foretold of a city to the south to be built where an eagle held a snake while perched on a cactus."

"You say that like you believe it." Perry sniped.

Jane twisted about. "It is the symbol on the Mexican flag to this day." She resumed examining the statue. "This has to be the exact piece that the Spanish searched for throughout the temples after the fall of Tenochtitlan. No wonder Cortés said he knew nothing of it. Many were tortured by those who had to account to the Spanish royal crown. After dozens of natives were killed without any clues to its location, its existence was presumed to be just a rumor."

"And who might this fellow be?" Apperson asked, pointing at a figurine with a man's face protruding from the mouth of a feathered dragon with two pearls as eyes.

"That must be Quetzalcoatl, the plumed serpent. The fair-skinned god of air whose legendary return from the east was exploited when mistaken for the Spaniards' arrival."

More artifacts caught her eyes: statuettes of other deities in gold and silver adorned with emeralds, pearls, quartz, and sapphires; carved and polished stone images of Aztec natives, dogs, and birds. She picked up a miniature infant child cut from jade and held it in her palm.

Over her shoulder, she saw Cole, who stood with his hands on his hips. At first, he appeared perturbed by her success, but the longer she looked, a grin could be detected on his face. She took it as a congratulatory smile. It was then she let out a long-held breath and realized her own success.

The light faded rapidly. Darkness fell like a curtain.

"We better get out of here while we can see," Cole ordered.

"But we can't leave this behind," declared Apperson.

"We'll make torches and come back. Now let's get."

Jane scampered behind Adela as the two women followed Cole and Perry through the tunnel. Once at the foot of the pyramid, she peered up to see the skull now only dimly lit, yet still casting enough light for the entire party to find the steps. Once the skull disappeared into the darkness, outer daylight served as a lighthouse guiding them to the mouth of the cave.

The overcast sky was the first thing she noticed. "The clouds blocked the light again." A glance to the west showed blue sky. "It looked like they'll pass quickly. We can go back in soon."

"I don't know how much time that'll give you down there," said Cole. "You said the sun had to be straight up over it. It ain't going to be like that long." He pointed to Adela and Apperson. "If they scrounge up enough sagebrush to make a fire and wood to use as torches, you can be down there all night."

"Capital idea, old man. I'll look straightaway." Apperson immediately began the descent to the floor of the gulch.

"Cancel that order!" Perry pointed to the west. Jane went to his side and Cole came next to her. She peered at dust rising in the distance. "I think our friends have made their return. I see more than a dozen riders."

Cole nodded. "And you can bet they're tracking us right to where we stand." He exhaled through billowed cheeks while scanning behind, to both sides, and in front. "How do you think they'll come at us?"

"They should try to flank our position and attack in a crossfire. It's the tactic I'd use." Perry looked to the top of the cave opening. "I gauge that a height of more than fifty feet from here. I wouldn't believe they'd attempt to leap down and risk falling to the bottom of the gulch. But it is the highest point with a clear line of sight. Therefore, that's where I'll be." He cradled the Mouton rifle. "We'll hold as long as we can. Just as the men of the Alamo."

"They all got killed," said Cole with disgust.

"We'll hope for a more favorable outcome. We haven't any other choice." After a moment, a grin broke the soldier's face. "Hey, Cole. Remember when we were ambushed by Satanta's Kiowa in Kansas?"

"I remember."

257

"What happened?" Jane asked, eagerly curious.

"The twelve of us repelled a band of a hundred," Perry said proudly.

"We had Spencer carbines," Cole argued. "They were shooting arrows. And it weren't a hundred, it was more like thirty, and we still lost five men."

"It was a hundred if it was one!"

"Damn you, Miles. To hear you tell it, Custer ain't dead."

"Don't ever speak the man's name in vain." They faced each other with shoulders pinned back.

"Would you two stop it!" shouted Jane, as she stood firmly between them. "We're under attack. Dispense your anger against those who are coming at us." She eyed both men, then they eyed each other.

"Fine by me," Cole said, marching past Perry.

A moment went by before the major moved. "I'll take my position."

Jane went to Cole. His drawn cheeks showed his concern. "I can't say he's wrong," he said, checking his gun's ammunition. "I don't look good. Take them other two and get as far inside as you can. Don't make a sound and stay put no matter what goes on up here."

"I say," Apperson blurted. "Can we reason with them, do you think? There's a fortune down there."

"You breathe one word of what's down there," Cole snarled, "and you'll end up with your throats cut." He glanced back at the approaching riders. "Now get on your way."

While Adela and Apperson hurried inside, Jane gave Cole a last look. He met her eyes only briefly, then took her arm and shoved her on her way. She took a few steps, stopped and peeked around the cave entrance once Cole's back was turned to witness the ensuing confrontation.

Crouched behind a small encrusted ridge, he steadied the pistol over his forearm and pulled back the hammer. The riders reined in their horses at the brim of the gulch. Comanches with rifles dismounted and moved down the same path that the party had used.

She edged farther around the entrance to see better when Cole's single gunshot broke the silence, startling her to retreat into the cave, but not before she saw a Comanche fall from the gulch wall while the rest quickly scattered about for cover.

"Señores," Gura's voice echoed. "Let us talk, not shoot."

"Throw all your guns in the middle of that sandbed," Cole yelled. "Then we'll talk."

"I think I will not do that. But I have another offer. Send out my wife, Adela, with my son. Then I will let the rest of you pass in peace."

Cole peered over his shoulder at Jane. His scowl showed his reaction to her not being farther inside. Jane quickly ducked into the cooler shadows only to stop upon seeing the frightened Mexican girl holding her child close to her chest. A moment passed while Jane thought about the cruel bargain being proposed outside.

"She ain't here," Cole shouted. "We sent her and the other woman and the old man back to the white man's camp at Langtry. Could be half way there by now."

A cackled laugh bounced off the walls. "I think you are lying to me, amigo. I didn't see any horse tracks from the wagon. I will kill you-all just for her. Send her to me."

Jane wrapped her arms around Adela awaiting Cole's reply.

"And you're just going to let us go?" he yelled.

"Of course. I am a man of my word."

"How about your friend Mouton? Make him the same deal?"

"He was not a man of his word."

"So you had me kill him for you." Jane sensed the anger growing in Cole's voice.

"Yes. That is why I admire you and wish to see you live."

"I think not," Cole yelled. "If you want to come see if the girl is here, you come right up this hill."

The two women huddled together. Fearful to leave the shadows again, Jane wondered if Cole meant what he said, allowing Gura to search for Adela. The answer came shortly after with the eruptions of gunfire. She flinched from the echoed blasts inside the cave.

Both women sank to their knees. Jane cringed with each shot, unsure whether either Cole or Major Perry was alive or dead. A meager illumination shined into her eye. Although dim, the skull reemerged from the darkness.

She rose helping Adela to stand. Apperson waved for them to follow him onto the staircase. They stepped down quickly, risking a fall off the slick surface. It was a far better fate than being captured by Gura and his men.

Once at the bottom, the three hastily found the paved pathway. Apperson went first through the tunnel, then Jane helped Adela, all while the sounds of the battle raging outside boomed like thunder around them. Once they were all past the overhang and careful to step over the fissures, they arrived once again at the foot of the Aztec temple.

Apperson stood as if mesmerized by the eyes of the golden idol. "We can't let this happen. This must be pure gold." he said, facing Jane. His sly grin was a sign to her that he wasn't thinking clearly. "We can't have come all this way just to have this taken from us."

"Lord Apperson, keep your voice down. It could echo and give away where we are." She prayed now that the clouds would return to cloak their location. However, the rays from the skull intensified, reflecting light off the gold calendar.

"We must hide it," he said and charged to the idol.

As she watched him attempt to move the heavy statue, she caught sight of a particular encryption on the calendar. Instantly, she recognized that it wasn't a calendar, but rather a codex, a manuscript depicting deities at war.

As her eyes darted to each individual hiero-glyphic, she saw the bottom image of a youthful man with open palms: Tezcatlipoca, the soul of the world. She drew the bodice cloth. It was the same encryption, except the area she couldn't trace was the Aztec god of the dead, meant to receive the souls of the temple. It was a warning.

"No! Stop!" she called and ran to Apperson. She grabbed at his shoulder but he wouldn't release his hold. "You mustn't move it. The codex is a admonition of the end of the world if the supreme god is destroyed."

"But I must have it," he said in delirium. Unable to wrestle his grasp free, she yanked at his arm. The idol dislodged and tilted toward him. Jane pushed Apperson aside, and the heavy statue toppled her to the floor. She crashed on her back, but the extended arms of the idol kept her from its crushing weight. Although alive, she lay pinned under the idol.

"Oh, my God! What have I done!" Apperson cried. He tugged at the statue, but could not budge it. "Forgive me, Jane. I'll get you out."

Her heart pounded. She pushed as he pulled, yet neither of their efforts moved the weight enough to free her. Adela shrieked. Apperson attempted another grasp and pushed in another direction, only to have his hand slip and fall prone on the floor. He appeared dazed at the simple task of rising.

Jane's eyes became irritated and her vision blurred. Although she'd pushed in short bursts, her muscles tingled and she felt fatigued and drowsy. It was then she realized the meaning of the codex. "Lord Apperson. You must leave. The air . . . is poisoned with gas."

The old man groggily got to his feet. "I'll get help." Adela took his arm to guide him and they exited into the tunnel.

Jane felt her eyes well up with tears. Her confused mind tried to focus on a solution, but she couldn't concentrate. Trapped under the idol, she hastened her own doom with each breath.

Chapter Nineteen

Three Comanches came up through the rocks. Cole fired, putting a red hole in the first one's chest. The other two dove back behind cover. So did Cole. "Do you see any more?" he yelled at Perry.

Several seconds passed without words. Cole flicked open the chamber gate on the Colt. A spin of the cylinder showed two spent cartridges. He reached behind him to pop fresh ones from his gunbelt, but before he could, Perry yelled.

"On the right!"

Cole rolled onto his knees, the barrel pointed in line with his eyes, his thumb cocking the hammer. A pair of figures moved between the rocks. He squeezed the trigger, but when the smoke blew by, the figures were gone and no blood stained the gulch walls. A quick scan showed no others. Again, he ducked behind his ridge shield. He flicked open the chamber gate and pushed out the spent shells. "How many you got left?"

"Three more magazines."

"How many forty-fives?"

"I reloaded the last six I had."

Cole removed two cartridges from his belt and slid them into the open cylinders. He reached around for more, but a ricochet spattered bits of stone and sand into eyes. He brushed his vision clear and twisted around in the shot's direction. Two other Comanches, rifles butted against their shoulders, charged up the hill.

Cole fired, hitting one in the gut. The other returned fire, the bullet whirring past Cole's head. Perry fired from behind, but the remaining Comanche still advanced, levered his action and shot. Cole cocked the Colt's hammer and squeezed the trigger, plugging the attacker in the chest who then collapsed within feet of the ridge.

Glancing to his right, Cole noticed a dead Mexican lay listless on the sand. "That your shot?"

"Who else?"

Cole continued to scan in front of him, bobbing his head between the tiny crevices of the ridge. The strategy against them was easily understood. Draw as much fire as possible to allow advances in position on the other flank. A missed shot meant an enemy was still alive and it was hard to kill two with one bullet. If he ran out of lead, he'd soon be shot full of it. The tactic was as old as fighting itself, one he'd rather use to his benefit instead of battling it and what scared him worse was that it seldom failed.

"Miles, throw me the Schofield." A few seconds went by before the gun dropped some ten feet away. Cole crept a couple of steps toward it, but that took him away from his cover. Two shots pelted the ground, spraying sand, chasing him back behind the ridge.

"Mr. Cole!" Apperson's cry came from the mouth of the cave and on the other side of the Schofield. "It's Jane! She needs you at once."

Cole kept his eyes open for any movement in front of him. "Get back inside, you damn fool."

"She's dying."

He arched around at the cave. "What?"

"She's trapped inside and poison gas is leaking into the cave. I'm terrified she'll be dead in minutes. You must get her out."

He already tried to move from cover and almost caught lead for it. The cave was double the distance and a loaded pistol lay in the middle. If he made it, the lost firing position would make Perry an easy target.

"Hurry," screamed Apperson.

Cole kept his eyes forward. Apperson's voice had echoed through the gulch. Gura likely was waiting for him to move.

"Clay!" Perry shouted. "Go get her. I'll cover you."

Cole took a deep breath. "One, two." He cocked the Colt and bolted. "Three!" Charging at the cave, he fired a wild shot at the rocks below. Two bullets flew over his head. He dove at the Schofield, snatched it with his left hand and rolled onto his knees. A Comanche with a rifle stood from cover. Reflex had Cole thumb the Colt's hammer back and fired, hitting his target in the forehead. Another blurred figure came from the left. A whir near his ear tore off his hat and he lost his balance. Flat on his back, bullets popped up dust near his boots. He fired the Colt, then the Schofield to stop a shooter from charging, but he couldn't see any coming at him nor if he hit one.

"Get up and move!" Cole glanced at the top of the cave's crown after Perry yelled. The major stood and aimed the Mouton rifle and fired. He pumped the action quicker than a drunk with a twitch. Sparks streamed a foot from the muzzle. Smoky spent casings spit out the side as the soldier swept the barrel from left to right.

Cole rose to his feet and sprinted to the mouth of the cave. A single Mexican sprung from the near rocks, but Cole squeezed the double action Schofield's trigger twice from his hip and the Mexican slumped behind the rocks.

"Come on, you red savages," Perry shouted as he kept shooting. The rapid barrage had left four bodies bleeding on the sandbed, but Perry still stood and fired.

"Miles, get down," Cole called.

A single blast stopped Perry from shooting. The rifle drooped to his hip. Two more shots exploded holes in the soldier's blouse. The rifle fell from his hand. For a moment he stood in a stupor staring blankly, then leaned forward and fell as if in a dive, but Cole knew there was no life left in the major's body. He lost sight of it falling to the bottom of the gulch.

The same fate would take him if kept watching, so Cole darted inside the cave. Apperson knelt next to the entrance. "Take this and shoot anything you see," he said, handing the Englishman the Schofield.

"But any sparks could ignite the gas. Everything would explode. She's at the temple."

Cole paid no mind to the warning as he scampered to the staircase. He paused enough to see a quivering Adela as she hid between the horses, then continued down the steps. Once at the bottom, he ran to the tiled path and into the tunnel. Quickly ducking the overhang and jumping the fissures, he entered the temple chamber.

Jane lay under the gold statue. Cole holstered the revolver and went to her. She wasn't breathing, but his fingers sensed a weak pulse. He clutched the idol's golden feathers. Driving his legs and grunting aloud, he shoved it off her. He took a breath and felt dizzy. His eyes began to burn.

The gold glistened brighter. In an instant, he recalled Apperson's warning of poison. A couple of blinks watered his eyes enough to focus on a beam of light shining into a fine point on the round calendar. The white light became blue. Cole remembered fires having been started with spectacles aiming sunlight into straw.

He lifted Jane over his shoulder and fought to keep his balance as he exited through the tunnel. When he was out of it, he ran past the brilliant glow atop the pyramid. "Get out! Mount up and get out!"

"Hello, senor," came a shout from atop the precipice. There Gura stood with a grip of Adela's arm. One of the two men behind him held a gun to Apperson's temple. "What do you have in here?"

Cole knew if he reached for iron, he surely would be shot. "Why don't you come down here and find out."

"I think I will. But first you give me your gun."

"I'll walk it up there to you," said Cole, feeling a sting to his eyes. He climbed up the steps. Once at the top, he handed Gura the Colt. "There's gold down there. Old Indian treasure. I guess you're the one who won it."

Gura huffed out laughter. "Why do you give it to me so easily?"

With each second gone, Cole knew Jane's life was passing. "The woman here needs help. The air in here . . . is too wet. She needs fresh air outside. I'll give you the treasure, if you let us go."

Gura's smile quickly became a scowl. He drew one of his pistols, cocked the hammer, and pointed it in Cole's face. "What if I just shoot you first?"

"Don't," Apperson groaned. The man guarding him shoved a pistol into Apperson's mouth.

"Well?" asked Gura. "I'm waiting for your answer."

"You best hurry," said Cole calmly. "The light in here only lasts a few more minutes. After that, it'll take you days to find it by torchlight."

Gura's eyes darted to the skull. As if considering the proposition, Gura nodded. He rambled in Mex at his two friends, then went toward the steps with Adela.

"Leave her here." Gura twisted around to Cole. "Them steps are slippery. Might risk her falling with that baby." Frustrated by the wisdom of Cole's words, Gura went down the steps without her, motioning one of his men to follow.

As the two Mexicans marched passed the pyramid, the light became blinding. Cole turned his back to the light and noticed the one guarding Apperson did the same. Now was the time.

Cole kicked the man to the ground, jarring the Colt loose. Cole picked it up and cocked the hammer at the same time as the guard. Cole squeezed the trigger, but the hammer fell without firing. In an instant, he realized he was out of bullets.

The guard raised his pistol, but the ensuing shot didn't come from his gun. The guard's head exploded with blood. Cole's eyes darted to Apperson, holding the Schofield, smoke wisping from the muzzle. "Never so alive!" muttered the Englishman.

Gura came running back to the steps.

"Let's ride!" Cole shouted. He hobbled past Apperson and Adela scrambling onto their horses. He threw Jane across his saddle, stepped into the stirrup, and slapped the palomino's rump. Whistles and screams had the animals charge from the cave. As Cole cleared out of the mouth of the cave, he spanked his mount and clung to the horn.

The ground rumbled. Almost shook from his grip, Cole peeked behind. The cave mouth filled with flame with the thrust of a giant cannon. Rocks shot from all around and fell like hail.

Once at the bottom of the gulch, Cole reined the palomino to a stop while Adela and Apperson rode by. He dragged Jane off the saddle, cradling her in his arms, and laid her on her back. She still wasn't breathing. He pressed his lips over hers and blew air into her mouth. With no reaction, he repeated the act.

Jane coughed and struggled to inhale. Finally she wheezed in a long breath. Her eyes blinked open, and once Cole was certain she focused on him, he grinned and laughed. She smiled slightly and nodded. An explosion drew his attention back to the cave. A long thin flame spiraled from the top like a tornado.

"*No!*" Apperson shouted as he ran toward the cave. "We must go back! We must go back!"

Cole tackled him to the dirt. Flames shot from the cave mouth and a jolt shook the ground. A blast of heated wind blew into Cole's face, forcing his eyes closed. Slowly, he peered through a tight squint. The fire was gone and so was the cave. In its place lay a sunken pile of boulders leveled by the blast, smoke rising through the stones.

Chapter Twenty

Jane rummaged through the rubble, looking for any sign, any hope of recovering what was lost beneath the rocks. Jagged boulders and crushed stones showed no prospect of their regaining access to the greatest exhibition of mankind's past. The tragic evidence before her tore away at her faith, slowly convincing her what lay below was surely pummeled into mere remnants of their once pristine form.

Her reflection became more personal. As she picked up a small rock, it seemed to represent what could have been. Amid the devastation, a wave of gratitude swarmed her soul. Her dreams had been shattered, but *she* was still alive in one piece. Her thoughts turned to those that didn't share the same fortune.

The image of Jeffers popped into her head.

The gracious gentleman would always be a fond memory. He continued his life of service to another to his own end without complaint. Although she didn't know him well, somehow it seemed fitting. It was a life chosen for him, a tradition of his upbringing. A parallel in history, she thought. The civilization that had drawn her to this spot also had those who nobly sacrificed themselves for the presumed greater good of others. The terrible difference was the anonymity of those 300 years before bore no comparison to the memory of a beloved friend. A silent prayer for his eternal peace would have to suffice as her appreciation of the debt.

Serge Mouton was another matter. He was no friend, but an opportunist preying on those who entrusted him with their secret. His death was no less horrible; however, as Jeffers's end was fitting, so too was the Belgian's just. There wasn't a prayer inside her to convey.

"What a terrible waste." Lord Apperson's voice behind her was a welcome reminder of what in her world still remained. "Take heart, Jane. All is not lost. We have a great deal to take from the discovery. The satisfaction of knowing that we found what others dismissed as rumor, for one. We will yet hold the trappings of this find, I assure you. We will give it another effort and we will be successful."

She smiled at his pompous boast. Yet, he was right. There was still a triumph to be salvaged, although it wasn't made of gold, but something more precious; her accomplishment. A woman in a man's world, attempting to establish a career where one's professional opinion was measured by the wealth of those whom invested in it. The failure wasn't hers. She had been right.

Nonetheless, without a single artifact to display, no provenance had been established. The gold of Cortés would likely remain whispered about in private circles just as it had been by the Spanish and all those since who had been captivated by the enigma and no one else. The accomplishment was indeed hers, and just as fatefully tragic, it would remain only hers alone.

"I suppose we should leave it for another day."

Apperson's remark brought Jane back to the present. Also, it brought to mind that there was one more casualty. She looked to the side. There, Cole walked in the distance toward a small pile of stone. Having barely known the military officer who joined the expedition with a different goal, she would leave his remembrance to the only one among the living capable of doing so.

With one more rock, Cole placed the final piece needed to complete the resting place of Major Miles Arthur Perry. The marker of crossed sticks cinched together with a strip of leather likely wouldn't last beyond the next stiff Texas breeze, but it was all that could be managed.

Not one for saying prayers, Cole removed his hat as he stood next to the monument. He recalled the times when he was certain he would be the one responsible for the need to bury the major, but never thought he would be the single pallbearer. No matter their battles in the past of words and lead, there still seemed a need for something to be said. Just what he wasn't sure.

Here lay a man devoted to duty. Even though it was well-known that Miles Perry often decided just what his duty was, even when it conflicted with orders, he was a patriot to his country. Just as with his idol, George Custer, Perry's ambition blinded him into believing he couldn't be killed. As it turned out, it was that ambition that not only cost him his life, but saved Cole's, a man who the major had hunted and might have led in parade to the firing squad.

He felt no sadness, but there was some regret. Miles Perry couldn't be mistaken for a friend, but he was a part of Cole's life. Although they didn't see things the same, they had decided to stand up to it together, tell their part of the same story, and rid both of them of the chain that linked them together for the last five years.

At that moment, Cole realized what he had to do. Perry just happened to be the body taking form of that which constantly shrouded his name. The major's passing wouldn't set the record straight. It had been left to him.

As he stepped toward Jane and Apperson, he remembered he hadn't said anything over the grave. He'd have to rely on the notion that dead spirits could read a fellow's mind. "I'm going to settle this for both of us, Miles. I hope they give you a fair deal, wherever you end up."

He went back to the horses, only glancing at the other bodies strewn about the dust. The increasing heat convinced him to let the good man above claim their souls and the varmints claim the rest. As he climbed over the rocks, Apperson, Jane, and Adela prepared the horses for the long ride back to Langtry.

Cole took the palomino's reins, but before he stepped into the stirrup, his eyes met those of the Mexican girl. It didn't seem the frightened stare as she'd always shown him. When he glanced at her baby in the basket strapped atop the horse, he recalled another memory. He opened his saddlebag and pulled out the shawl.

He walked around the palomino and without a word offered it to her. As she took it from him, she stood on her toes and kissed his cheek, then rattled off words in her lingo. Cole smiled at her, turning to Jane for what was said.

"She'll always think of you as the one in the cloth whenever she looks at it. I believe she means the armored knight."

When he looked back at Adela, she wore a smile. It was the first time he could recall her aiming it at him. He nodded his appreciation and mounted his horse.

"We haven't given up, Mr. Cole," said Apperson. "As soon as we regroup our resources, we're planning on recovering what was lost. I'll pay you as soon as we happen along a bank that will take a draft. We'd very much like for you to remain with us. I'd be willing to double the amount for your service this time."

"Well that's a mighty hard offer to turn down, Mr. Apperson. But, I believe I'll pass. This whole business has taught me something. Whatever you got planned on doing someday, you best get at while you have the chance. I swore to myself that I wasn't going to end up like them on the sand. Least not in Texas." He looked to Jane. "Me and Perry made up our minds to get this whole mess behind us. I guess in a way I owe him that, and I guess I owe myself that too. I'm going to head back East. There's a woman who's fighting awful hard to clear my name, and I'd hate to do anything to get in the way of that." He tipped his hat at the women and nudged his horse. "I wish all of you the best of luck. I hope you find what you're looking for."

Jane gave a last look into his eyes as he passed. "I hope you find what you're looking for as well."

An early snow fell over the harbor, an oddity for September. An apt sign for the news she'd learned earlier in the day. Claire stepped away from the window. The nightmare that had lasted for two months had finally ended, only to begin another.

This loss was not just hers, but the entire country's. A man who had promised much was gone. It was a tragedy for any man to die, especially one with a family. His death had robbed others of their dreams. She fought to put her selfish feelings from her mind. Nevertheless, the hope she felt was so near now was just as far away as when she began her personal mission.

She went to sit on the bench in the foyer where the newspaper lay. To begin anew would take far more effort than before. Her father's condition hadn't improved and her mother's constant bewilderment over what next to do had left Claire as head of the family. It must have been the same position Mr. Arthur had found himself in the last two months. Still, just as the nation had to continue, so would she. There was still much to be done.

Young Stuart mastering his steps drew her attention. It should be a delightful time in both their lives and there were surely more to come. Her son personified the debt she owed one man. His gleeful infant smile renewed her resolve that her son would one day meet Clay Cole. The next day she would begin again, but today belonged to Stuart.

As she rose, she resolved that the day's headline of the death of President Garfield wasn't going to spoil her refreshed spirit. "I'm coming, darling. I'll be there. I'll always be there."

MAN WITHOUT MEDICINE

CYNTHIA HASELOFF

Daha-hen's name in Kiowa means Man Without Medicine. Before his people were forced to follow the peace road and live on a reservation, Daha-hen was one of the great Kiowa warriors of the plains, fabled for his talent as a horse thief. But now Daha-hen is fifty-three and lives quietly on the edge of the reservation raising horses. When unscrupulous white men run off his herd, the former horse thief finds himself in pursuit of his own horses and ready to make war against the men who took them. Accompanying him on his quest is Thomas Young Man, a young outcast of the Kiowa people. During the course of their journey, Daha-hen adopts Thomas and teaches him the ways of the Kiowa warrior. But can Daha-hen teach his young student enough to enable them both to survive their trek—and the fatal confrontation that waits at the end of it?

____4581-8 $4.50 US/$5.50 CAN

Dorchester Publishing Co., Inc.
P.O. Box 6640
Wayne, PA 19087-8640

Please add $1.75 for shipping and handling for the first book and $.50 for each book thereafter. NY, NYC, and PA residents, please add appropriate sales tax. No cash, stamps, or C.O.D.s. All orders shipped within 6 weeks via postal service book rate. Canadian orders require $2.00 extra postage and must be paid in U.S. dollars through a U.S. banking facility.

Name_____

Address_____

City_____ State_____ Zip_____

I have enclosed $_____ in payment for the checked book(s).

Payment <u>must</u> accompany all orders. ☐ Please send a free catalog.

CHECK OUT OUR WEBSITE! www.dorchesterpub.com

THE HUNTING OF TOM HORN

WILL HENRY

Lively, action-packed, exciting, this is a collection of short masterpieces by one of the West's greatest storytellers. The characters in these tales—be they cowboy or bounty hunter, preacher or killer—are living, breathing people, people whose stories could be told only by a master like Will Henry.

___4484-6 $5.50 US/$6.50 CAN

Dorchester Publishing Co., Inc.
P.O. Box 6640
Wayne, PA 19087-8640

Please add $1.75 for shipping and handling for the first book and $.50 for each book thereafter. NY, NYC, and PA residents, please add appropriate sales tax. No cash, stamps, or C.O.D.s. All orders shipped within 6 weeks via postal service book rate. Canadian orders require $2.00 extra postage and must be paid in U.S. dollars through a U.S. banking facility.

Name_____
Address_____
City_____State_____Zip_____
I have enclosed $_____ in payment for the checked book(s).
Payment <u>must</u> accompany all orders. ❑ Please send a free catalog.
CHECK OUT OUR WEBSITE! www.dorchesterpub.com

WILL HENRY

THE LAST WARPATH

"The most critically acclaimed Western writer of this or any other time!"
—Loren D. Estleman

The battle between the U.S. Cavalry and the wild-riding Cheyenne, lords of the North Prairie, rages across the Western plains for forty years. The white man demands peace or total war, and the Cheyenne will not pay the price of peace. Great leaders like Little Wolf and Dull Knife know their people are meant to range with the eagle and the wolf. The mighty Cheyenne will fight to be free until the last warrior has gone forever upon the last warpath.

**FIVE-TIME WINNER OF THE
GOLDEN SPUR AWARD**

___4314-9 $4.50 US/$5.50 CAN
Dorchester Publishing Co., Inc.
P.O. Box 6640
Wayne, PA 19087-8640

Please add $1.75 for shipping and handling for the first book and $.50 for each book thereafter. NY, NYC, and PA residents, please add appropriate sales tax. No cash, stamps, or C.O.D.s. All orders shipped within 6 weeks via postal service book rate. Canadian orders require $2.00 extra postage and must be paid in U.S. dollars through a U.S. banking facility.

Name_____
Address_____
City_____State_____Zip
I have enclosed $_____ in payment for the checked book(s).
Payment <u>must</u> accompany all orders. ❏ Please send a free catalog.

WILL HENRY

YELLOWSTONE KELLY

Yellowstone Kelly is an Indian fighter and scout like no other. The devil-may-care Irishman can pick off hostiles and quote the classics with equal ease and accuracy. Even the mighty Sioux fear him. Most of them. Sitting Bull's main war chief, the dreaded Gall, fears no man, and Kelly has something of his that the warrior will gladly kill to get back—his woman.

___4364-5 $4.99 US/$5.99 CAN

Dorchester Publishing Co., Inc.
P.O. Box 6640
Wayne, PA 19087-8640

Please add $1.75 for shipping and handling for the first book and $.50 for each book thereafter. NY, NYC, and PA residents, please add appropriate sales tax. No cash, stamps, or C.O.D.s. All orders shipped within 6 weeks via postal service book rate. Canadian orders require $2.00 extra postage and must be paid in U.S. dollars through a U.S. banking facility.

Name_____
Address_____
City_____State_____Zip_____
I have enclosed $_____ in payment for the checked book(s).
Payment <u>must</u> accompany all orders. ☐ Please send a free catalog.

WILL HENRY

WHO RIDES WITH WYATT

"Some of the best writing the American West can claim!"
—Brian Garfield, Bestselling Author of Death Wish

They call Tombstone the Sodom in the Sagebrush. It is a town of smoking guns and raw guts, stage stick-ups and cattle runoffs, blazing shotguns and men bleeding in the streets. Then Wyatt Earp comes to town and pins on a badge. Before he leaves Tombstone, the lean, tall man with ice-blue eyes, a thick mustache and a long-barreled Colt becomes a legend, the greatest gunfighter of all time.

BY THE FIVE-TIME WINNER OF THE GOLDEN SPUR AWARD

___4292-4 $3.99 US/$4.99 CAN

Dorchester Publishing Co., Inc.
P.O. Box 6640
Wayne, PA 19087-8640

Please add $1.75 for shipping and handling for the first book and $.50 for each book thereafter. NY, NYC, and PA residents, please add appropriate sales tax. No cash, stamps, or C.O.D.s. All orders shipped within 6 weeks via postal service book rate. Canadian orders require $2.00 extra postage and must be paid in U.S. dollars through a U.S. banking facility.

Name_____
Address_____
City_____ State_____ Zip_____
I have enclosed $_____ in payment for the checked book(s).
Payment <u>must</u> accompany all orders. ❑ Please send a free catalog.

CHIRICAHUA

"Some of the best writing the American West can claim!"
—Brian Garfield, Bestselling Author of
Death Wish

Led by the dreaded Geronimo and Chatto, a band of Chiricahua Apache warriors sweep up out of Mexico in a red deathwind. Their vow–to destroy every white life in their bloody path across the Arizona Territory. But between the swirling forces of white and red hatred, history sends a lone Indian rider named Pa-nayo-tishn, The Coyote Saw Him, crying peace–and the fate of the Chiricahuas and all free Apaches is altered forever.

The Spur Award–winning Novel of the West
___4266-5 $4.50 US/$5.50

Dorchester Publishing Co., Inc.
P.O. Box 6640
Wayne, PA 19087-8640

Please add $1.75 for shipping and handling for the first book and $.50 for each book thereafter. NY, NYC, and PA residents, please add appropriate sales tax. No cash, stamps, or C.O.D.s. All orders shipped within 6 weeks via postal service book rate. Canadian orders require $2.00 extra postage and must be paid in U.S. dollars through a U.S. banking facility.

Name_____
Address_____
City_____ State_____ Zip_____
I have enclosed $_____ in payment for the checked book(s).
Payment <u>must</u> accompany all orders. ❑ Please send a free catalog.

WILL HENRY

THE CROSSING

By the Bestselling Author of *The Bear Paw Horses*

Jud is the son and grandson of famous Southern generals. He was reared in the genteel Virginia traditions of his widowed mother, but life on a Texas ranch has molded him in the harsh ways of the frontier. In the deadly Confederate campaign to secure the region, Jud sees brave men fall with their guns blazing or die from naked fear. But he is of better stock than most, and he'll be damned if he'll betray the land—and the woman—he loves just to save his own worthless hide.

_4084-0 $4.99 US/$5.99 CAN

Dorchester Publishing Co., Inc.
P.O. Box 6640
Wayne, PA 19087-8640

Please add $1.75 for shipping and handling for the first book and $.50 for each book thereafter. NY, NYC, and PA residents, please add appropriate sales tax. No cash, stamps, or C.O.D.s. All orders shipped within 6 weeks via postal service book rate. Canadian orders require $2.00 extra postage and must be paid in U.S. dollars through a U.S. banking facility.

Name_____
Address_____
City_____State_____Zip_____
I have enclosed $_____ in payment for the checked book(s).
Payment <u>must</u> accompany all orders. ☐ Please send a free catalog.